SMALL
BLUE
W🌍RLD

SMALL BLUE WORLD

STEVEN LEE CLIMER

FRACTURED MIRROR

ISBN: 978-1-7352171-5-4 (Paperback)
ISBN: 978-1-7352171-6-1 (Hardcover)

Library of Congress Control Number: 2021933089

Any references to historical events, real people, or real places are used fictitiously. Names, characters, and places are products of the author's imagination.

Book design by Allison Chernutan.
Earth image by photographeeasia.
Planets image by Freepik.

Printed in the United States of America.

First printing edition 2021.

emily@fracturedmirrorpublishing.com
Fractured Mirror Publishing
Knoxville, Tennessee

www.fracturedmirrorpublishing.com

THE EARTH HAS BECOME
THE ULTIMATE BATTLE GROUND...

EPIS⬤DE ONE

The Bloodstream of the Universe

Phineas Fletcher, **Professor** *Phineas Fletcher, gripped his* remarkable pocket-watch, also called an *aperture*, so tightly his fingernail beds turned white. He'd never been this nervous or stressed in hundreds of years. His eyes darted from the aperture to the pool of shadows on the abandoned factory floor. The watch was a tool of necessity, crafted in antiquity and handed down amongst his sect from professor to assistant for centuries. Normally, a professor would receive their aperture when they were no longer an acolyte, but his was more special than other apertures used by the Scholars. Eventually he would hand it down to his assistant, but until then he was its sole master.

At the moment, however, the pool of shadows was his most urgent objective. It wasn't the shadow itself, but what was inside it. She had been in there far too long.

"You are more nervous than a long-tailed cat in a room full

of rocking chairs," Poppy said in her high, girlish voice. "Do you think she'll make it out?"

"Of course," he glanced at the nine-year-old girl in a powder blue dress and patent-leather shoes standing nearby. "I wouldn't have sent her if I thought she wasn't ready."

"The Veil is curious," said Poppy. "There's no telling how it will receive someone coming through for the first time."

"It's not Carmen's first time with the Veil. She's been on that side many times before."

"But not in combat. She's only been there to explore and become familiar with the nature of the Veil. And we both know the Veil is about as predictable as a cobra."

"Can you be quiet, please?" He turned a few of the strange buttons on his watch. "I'm not able to really track her. I don't know where she is. Is she close?"

"I wonder if she will ever come back," chuckled Poppy.

"Be quiet, or I will never help lift your curse."

Poppy kicked him swiftly in the shin. "Fuck you. How would you like being trapped in the body of a little girl for 400 years. I'm *not* happy, and you said you would fix it."

"I'm not a miracle worker, and you earned that curse as I recall. My offer to help you was out of the kindness of my heart."

"Bullshit. You need me." Sullenly, she crossed her arms. "And if there was another person I thought could help me, I'd be gone in a flash."

"It's not a question of *could*, it's a question of *would*. No one —but me—is willing to help you."

"Aren't you worried she isn't going to make it back?"

"No, I have faith that she will."

"Maybe this pretty *señorita* is not who you think she is. You've been wrong before."

"I have been wrong before, I'll admit it. But the truth was always revealed long before this point. The Veil rejected the others far earlier. Carmen has made it further than any of them."

"Well, from my brief observance and unscientific calculations, she has about 2 minutes before the Veil consumes that sweet Latina soul. Tick tock, Doc," she laughed.

"You love to taunt me, don't you?"

"It's all I got, Doc." Poppy grabbed his sleeve.

"Shut up and look!" She pointed to the pool of shadows.

Two hands emerged from the shadows like a person pulling themselves up after an exhaustive swim. It took all of her strength to haul herself back into her world, sodden with perspiration. All her energy was drained, it was clear. The young woman extended her arms, locked her elbows, and scrambled from the shadow to collapse on the edge.

"Help me!" Fletcher shouted to Poppy as he ran to render assistance.

Together, they pulled the young woman free of the pool like a drowning victim. Fletcher checked her over. She was breathing, but was nearly unconscious.

"Carmen, can you hear me? Are you okay?"

She lifted her heavy head like a drunk, "I'm okay. Am I dead? I feel dead."

"You're not dead, not yet," said Poppy.

"You are not helping matters," said Fletcher. "Get her to safety, there's no telling what could be after her."

"All by myself?" complained Poppy. "I'm a nine-year-old, well in a nine-year-old's body, how am I supposed to lift that heifer of a girl by myself."

"Carmen is far from a heifer and you're a 400-year-old witch. I know what you can do, and what you cannot. So, make with the magic and get her to the tattoo shop."

"Thanks for pointing that out, and I'm 409, to be exact. In the meantime, what will you be doing?"

"I have to see Miss Venus. I have some suspicions. Carmen Perez may not be our only concern."

"She's not Nemesis." Poppy could read his mind. "Nemesis is not coming back any time soon."

He turned to the girl. "You don't know that," snapped Fletcher. "There's going to be much more. I feel it." He stood and looked at the aperture with its tiny metal cogs and dials. "Please get a message to Mr. Nash and tell him to meet me at the museum this evening."

"You know he hates to be summoned."

"He's my neophyte, he will do as he is told, or he'll never get this aperture." Fletcher then stalked from the abandoned factory.

The afternoon was rather pleasant in contrast to the ordeal in the abandoned factory with Carmen Perez. Fletcher looked across the green, city park in the *Campus Martius* district of downtown Detroit. The agreeable late spring weather attracted all sorts of downtown dwellers in the resurrected heart of the city: hipsters, artists, career girls, old executives. Then, at the far end of the park, he saw the familiar ice cream truck.

With big candy-looking marquee movie light bulbs encircling a red and white striped awning, there were no customers at the window of the colorful van. All sorts of sweet treat names were painted on the sides in lurid fluorescent colors that looked more impressive at night. He walked up to the window and tapped lightly on the stainless-steel counter.

"Why Professor Fletcher, as I live and breathe," Venus stood from a rickety stool, "I have missed you."

Fletcher smiled, "It's good to see you again, too." He leaned against the side of the van, "You look well."

She laughed, more of an ancient cackle, "You are so full of shit. I love it."

Miss Venus was so old she defied the term. There was no way to even guess at her proper age for even she stopped keeping track of her birthdays centuries ago. She wore a colorful blue paisley bandana wrapped and knotted around her skull. Her dark skin, withered and wrinkled like an old brown paper bag, contrasted with the bright chunky silver jewelry and beads hanging from her coat-wire neck.

"Is the cotton candy fresh?" asked Fletcher.

"Sure is. I spun it not more than ten minutes ago. But I got something better for you, honey." She pulled a bottle of dark liquor from below the window and put it on the counter along with two shot glasses. "Just got this: *Pappy Van Winkle*. And this is the private stuff, not the 23. This bottle be old."

Fletcher grinned broadly. "Oh, my sweetheart, I adore you. Where did you get it?"

"Let's just say someone owed me something."

"Everyone owes you something." Fletcher took the bottle in hand and gave the cap a twist, breaking the seal. "Shall I pour?"

"Be my guest. With these shaky hands, I'd likely spill it all over the place."

Fletcher poured three fingers into each shot glass. He offered one to his ancient companion, and he took the remaining one for himself. They clinked rims and both shot back the bourbon. She laughed at him as he reacted by sucking wind through his bared teeth.

"Smooth," he grimaced. "That's surely not the stuff you get at the local liquor store."

"No, it isn't," she smiled. "Now pour us up another while you tell me what you want."

He obliged. "Do you remember the plane crash about 16 years ago? The one that literally dropped from the sky on take-off, killing everyone except one little boy?" He slid the shot to her.

"Yes, I do."

"What do you know about that little boy?"

Together they took the shot. "Well, he isn't little anymore. He's a strapping young man with a promising future in sports, from what I hear."

"That's not what I want to know, Miss Venus, you know that." He leaned closer. "What is he?"

"He's *earthborne*. He is not *skyborne* or *starborne* as you may suspect." Venus reached for a bag of popcorn and began to munch as she talked. "He is indestructible, too."

"What's his name?"

"Ray Kellan. He is a nice young man with a doting adoptive mama."

"What do you know about the plane crash itself?"

"Only that a rare bolt of lightning on a sunny morning exploded the fuel tanks on take-off."

"Hmmm, *skyborne* mischief."

Miss Venus nodded. "True. They were trying to assassinate the baby, but they didn't know his nature. They killed his mother, though. She was his only living relative. No one could find out anything about her, or him, and eventually he was adopted out and given a new identity. No information on the father, either."

Fletcher reached for some popcorn. "Was the adoption your doing?"

"A lot of people owe me favors, but I owe my fair share, too. Some were called in, but I arranged things so the baby could grow up peacefully."

"Why did they want him dead?" asked Fletcher.

"Good question, and no one really knows that I can reckon. "

"Well someone wanted him dead." Fletcher paused, thinking. "It's not like there are *newbornes* everyday of any kind. Births of *newbornes* are rare."

"Perhaps, the *skyborne* did not want to see a new *earthborne* —it would increase the numbers of one over the other."

"What if he was *starborne*? What if you're wrong?"

"He is not, I am sure. I have heard nothing, and *starbornes* have little regard for *earthborne* folk. They consider them beneath everyone. They do not stay on this small blue world for long. They can be uppity."

"True," Fletcher poured one more shot. "Would you like another?"

"Yes, of course." Miss Venus put the popcorn aside, "But Ray Kellan is not the most interesting part of this."

"Oh?" Fletcher's attention sharpened. "Something more?"

"Not something more, but *someone* more. Ray was not the only *newborne* that year. A baby girl named Calliope Garner. *Starborne*."

"Where is she?" He took his shot.

Miss Venus took hers. "Calliope is transferring to Ray's high school this week. I made arrangements with Calliope's parents who are very worried about her temper. And her violent outbursts. I believe, as do her parents, that Ray may be the only one who can temper and contain her. I took the liberty of describing Ray, but not in too much detail."

"Interesting…." He turned his shot glass over, signaling he was done. "I can't wait until that storyline plays out, but right now I have to deal with Carmen Perez—and if our dear friend Nemesis has indeed returned to grace us with her presence from inside Carmen."

"Nemesis," laughed Miss Venus. "I haven't heard that name in a long time, but I suppose it is about time for her to show up. No one else will believe you. Ah, but times are different, there are a few who are expecting her, and no doubt they are prepared."

"The Wire?"

Miss Venus nodded. "Yes. You know them all too well."

He fiddled with his pocket watch. "That's the truth. I suppose I need to be getting to the museum. I have other irons in the fire."

"Do you think you may be playing with fire by getting immature teenagers involved in your schemes?"

"They're not schemes. And they're not ordinary teenagers. Well, not in the sense that they are *earthborne*, *skyborne*, or *starborne*."

"Just don't get them killed, can you do that?" laughed Miss Venus.

"I will try my best."

"One last thing," Venus' face darkened. "Were you going to tell me about Carmen Perez?"

Self-consciously, he looked away. "How did you know?"

"Phineas, do you even have to ask that?" Venus touched his hands, "This girl, you think it is Nemesis? Why?"

"I don't know," he replied. "All the signs say—*maybe*."

"You don't sound too sure of yourself. That's not like you. If it is Nemesis, then you know something bigger than all of us is about to happen. Do you think she is set to return after all this time?"

"Have there been this many *newbornes* before?"

"Not in a very long time."

"I guess no one knows then." He winked at her and left the ice cream truck for other obligations.

"Here we go again." Kendall sighed and looked across at his best friend, Peaches. "The history junkie!"

"Be quiet. Maybe if you were a little more in tune with the world you would have a plan after graduation."

Kendall and PJ (never call her by her full name) had been friends since 2nd grade when they fought over who got to dress up as the princess during free time. Kendall won and thus began his tortured ride through school as Ken Doll. It didn't help matters when he came out of the closet in 8th grade, but was surprised when no one was surprised. He may have been oblivious, but everyone else had known for years. Even his best friend PJ, who came out a month later as lesbian, knew. The taunting and teasing was momentary for the school had strict policies against bullying, but no one really cared that they were gay.

"What has got you so interested, then?" He fussed with his bleached blonde hair. "I want to go to the gym, you know, get my fitness on. And I need a new look for this hair."

"In a minute." PJ was engrossed in the story. "If you'd stop bleaching it, it will probably look better."

"I think you are the only person on Earth who still reads a newspaper. Why not just pull it up on your phone?"

"It's not the same." She glared over the page. "Now shut it so I can read the story if you wanna go workout. I'm not going until I'm done."

"Whatever, Peaches Jean. You could read it on your phone while you did cardio—like normal a human being."

She snapped the paper down. "I told you to never call me that. I'll beat you senseless."

"Promises, promises." Kendall fiddled with the empty coffee cup in front of him. "God, you are so old."

She sneered as only PJ Butler could, like a pitbull that could eat another pitbull for breakfast—who'd already eaten another pitbull for breakfast. "In case you want to know…apparently in one of the numerous archeological digs around Cairo, that's in Egypt—cuz I know you don't know that—something unusual was discovered. It seems that a pile of more than a thousand skulls was found in a pit beneath an ancient temple around Heliopolis—the city of the sun god Ra. Two experts were discussing it. One said it was evidence of dark rituals that support the legend of *Apep* who killed all the adults in ancient Cairo. The other said it was nothing more than a mass grave of plague victims."

"Boring." Kendall stood up. He wasn't very tall, but he was compact and muscular from years of swimming and gymnastics. "You can get your fill of weird at the museum later. God only knows why someone would want to be an intern there."

"God only knows why someone would want to work at Hollister. No one shops there anymore."

"Hot guys, that's why."

PJ rolled her eyes. "Don't be so lewd."

"That's your big word of the day, grandma. No more. Come on, let's go."

"Why are you in such a rush?" Then her eyes lit up. "*Oh*, because Daniel is at the gym right now."

"Whatever."

"He's my cousin, Kendall. He's not gay."

"Well I wouldn't complain if he was."

She put the paper down. "Fine, let's go. I promised Dr. Fletcher I would be at the museum to help him unpack and catalog some new stuff."

"Oh, sorry for yawning."

"You didn't."

"I was yawning in my mind."

PJ smacked him in the back of the head as they left the small coffee shop.

EPIS🌐DE TWO

The Whirlpool of Life

The Detroit Metropolitan Museum of History and Art was world class. PJ passed the security check with her badge and made her way through the labyrinth of a museum. The Metro specialized in Egyptian artifacts and exhibits, and Dr. Fletcher was one of the foremost experts on antiquity in the country. He also taught at the local university in the Anthropology Department. In fact, it was PJ's excellent grades that allowed her to take his college course as a high school student and get connected with Dr. Phineas Fletcher in the first place.

PJ turned the corner past a vast collection of Renaissance oil paintings, and down a hallway that could easily be missed if it wasn't purposely sought out. At the far end was a series of old art deco doors that reflected the time period when the main building was built.

She opened the last door. "Hi, Dr. Fletcher. Sorry, I'm late."

Fletcher was engrossed in some documents as he always was. "Hello, PJ. You're not late. Right on time. I just got here myself."

"So, what's up?"

He put down the papers. He was a strikingly handsome older man with short silver hair. Dr. Fletcher was also an avid cyclist, and he often did *Tough Mudder* runs and *Warrior Dashes*. He was one of those older men who ceased aging, at least to her, and just became more refined and improved. She had no idea how old he even was.

"A large box of artifacts unexpectedly arrived today. I wasn't expecting them for several weeks, but apparently, they cleared Customs quickly." He slid it towards PJ, "I just started going over the manifest and packing list, but these things need to be cataloged. Depending on what is in here, we could possibly use them in the new exhibit that opens at the end of the month."

"Good timing, then," said PJ.

"Maybe. I'm still puzzled why Dr. Khalifa sent them so quickly."

"Let me get to work on them." PJ reached for a catalog sheet. "I won't put numbers on them just yet until you're done with the manifest."

"One day you're going to make an awesome curator—if that is what you want to be."

She hesitated with her response. "I don't know. Maybe…"

"I thought you liked this work."

"I do, but…"

"Well, you are young. You will have a lot of opportunities. I wanted to be a knight, and now I'm an anthropologist." He grinned. "Imagine me as a knight."

"Actually, I could see that—if we lived in a time where there were knights." She laughed.

Dr. Fletcher grinned. "Thanks for humoring me."

Suddenly the door opened and Margaret, the department secretary, appeared. She seemed more flustered than usual, like a cat who had their fur stroked backward, and she tapped nervous fingers on the side of her pencil skirt. "Dr. Fletcher, we have a problem."

"What is it?"

"One of the custodians damaged some pottery being prepped for the exhibit."

The muscle in his jaw pulsed. It was the only way to tell if Dr. Fletcher was angry or stressed. "Let me see." As he followed Margaret, he paused to address PJ. "Keep working on those, and I'll be right back."

She acknowledged him with a nod and turned her attention to the box. It was full of packing peanuts so it meant the artifacts would be small. PJ wondered if they were jewels or any other things of value. She remembered a few months ago when she was the first to touch a diamond encrusted bracelet supposedly worn by an obscure Egyptian queen. Grabbing handfuls of peanuts, PJ uncovered the first item. It was a tarnished, old piece of bronze. She wasn't sure what it was, but it looked ceremonial in nature and looked damaged on one side. PJ wrote down the description, carefully noting every little blemish and mark. She would also have to take photos but that was a later step in the process. Dr. Fletcher was finicky on how he liked things done.

There were a few more mundane items, but then something quite peculiar was revealed. PJ recognized it immediately as a crescent moon-shaped knife about five inches long used in rituals. It was called a *Khonshu*. She placed it on the table in front of her and scrutinized the markings. The blade was a little damaged but in remarkably good shape for something so old. The handle had clear hieroglyphs on it, but PJ didn't know what they meant. There was a series of five that were largely square, but each had a different placement of dashes and swirls. Dr. Fletcher surely would, though. Then out of curiosity, PJ took a piece of paper out of the notebook she was using. The *Khonshu* sliced the paper like a razor brand new out of the package.

"Wow."

Just then Dr. Fletcher walked back in. "Wow, what?"

"Huh?" PJ looked up at him.

"Wow, what? You said 'wow' when I walked in."

"This knife," she held it up so he could see it, "it's still sharp enough to cut paper like scissors."

"Let me see that." Dr. Fletcher took it and held it up close to his eyes. "Strange…"

"What's strange?"

"These markings…" He turned it. The manifest was nearby, and he grabbed it. "These hieroglyphs are not common…" With the packing list in one hand and the knife in the other, he was comparing something. Suddenly, his eyes grew big and concerned. "PJ, I have to take care of something important." His jaw muscle was jumping. "Can you leave, and I will call you later?"

"What's wrong? What is it?" She strained to see the manifest. "What does it say?"

"Nothing of concern. This knife must be placed in a separate private collection. In fact, probably everything in the box."

"I haven't gone through it all yet."

"I will finish it, don't worry."

"Dr. Fletcher, I know that is a *Khonshu*."

"Yes, it is. Good observation. They were quite common in the palaces and temples." His jaw muscle was still twitching. "Well if you will excuse me." He grabbed the box and left the room.

"Wait!" PJ called after him as he walked down the hall a bit further and went into one of the other rooms with frosted glass. He shut the door without even acknowledging that she was still questioning him.

"Damn, that was rude."

It was not the first time Fletcher had shown up at the shop and directed Cleo to watch over an unconscious person and telling her to not let them die. The girl over whom she watched was beautiful. She was young, dark hair, Latina. Her body was small, but lean and quite capable of protecting herself. The fact she was still alive after crossing the shadows into the Veil was a testament to that. The girl stirred, grimaced with discomfort, and her eyes tightly squeezed shut. Cleo placed her ivory-cool palm on the girl's forehead. Closing her eyes, she inhaled and envisioned the girl's pain. In her mind, Cleo harnessed it, soothed it, calmed it down, and claimed as much as she could of it into her own body. The girl relaxed beneath her comforting touch.

At the door, Jesse Nash stood and watched. He was the owner of the tattoo shop, which was much more than a tattoo shop, and also the apprentice to Dr. Fletcher. Cleo was so gentle; he was not. To him, she appeared as breakable as porcelain cups, but that was underestimating her. Cleo was ancient as were all surviving oracles from the old days.

"Her name is Carmen Perez," Nash softly stated.

"Thank you, I didn't know."

"Another body dump by Fletcher? Did he 'miscalculate' again?

"Not exactly," Cleo stood up. "This is so very difficult to see. Her future is entwined with all of us."

Nash took off his leather jacket to reveal maps of tattoos on his arms, beneath his tight black t-shirt, and partway up his neck. He looked very tired. "Somehow I already knew that."

Cleo laughed, "You don't need a fortune teller to see that one."

"So true." He walked over to the girl and looked down in her face. "It's a miracle she is alive from what I understand."

"Not a miracle. This one is quite durable."

"He thought that the last two times he found a blind girl who had quick reflexes. It didn't make them live longer, now did it?"

Cleo paused. She knew exactly what Nash was thinking. "You have to let it go. You are not responsible for Amy's death. If anyone is responsible, it is Fletcher, but he is who he is."

"I know." Nash put his hand on Carmen's soft hair. "Do you think…?"

"I don't know. It's too hard to read at this time." She looked down at Carmen as well, "This one is much stronger than Amy and Sarah put together."

"Do you think he is losing it, seriously?" Nash grabbed her hand, "You must see something."

Cleo pulled away from him, "Shouldn't you be going to meet Dr. Fletcher at the museum?"

"I got some time," he replied. "Cleo, please, I don't want to see another girl die because he thinks it's…"

"…Nemesis?"

"Yeah, Nemesis."

"It isn't Nemesis." Cleo said. "Now go or you will be late. You know how he is about punctuality."

Nash laughed, "You got that right. Okay, but you will tell me if you know anything, right?"

"I will." She watched him leave the room and heard the door shut. "When the time is right."

Cleo turned her attention back to Carmen, the sweet blind girl Fletcher thought was the vessel of Nemesis. She laid hands on the girl, willing the energy of time to reveal all its secrets. The clouds surrounding her were swirled, pink, blue, green, not mixing, not forming images. Suddenly, the clouds cleared as if a stiff summer breeze blew them away.

Carmen opened her eyes, clear brown eyes. "Hello, Dione."

"Nemesis," gasped Cleo. "My lady." Cleo bowed her head and kissed Carmen's hand. "Oh, how I have missed you."

"And I you, my love." Carmen pulled Cleo close and kissed her deeply, passionately. "I have waited 500 years to kiss you again."

Tears streamed down Cleo's face. "I was too afraid to think it could be you."

"Oh, Dione, it is me. It's time for me to come back to mortal men."

"You are in the body of a young woman named Carmen. She is your vessel. But she is healing from her time in the Veil.

Fletcher took her in there too soon."

"Fletcher…" The name lingered on her lips, "…yes he did."

"You are the reason she survived, isn't it?"

"If I hadn't taken over, she would have died and I would not be here now. It was supposed to be this way. You know this, my oracle."

Cleo smiled, "I am so glad you are here."

"Me too, but it is not time for me to emerge. There are so many things happening that you may not see, and I like this girl, this vessel. She needs nurturing, from the inside. She is strong and fierce but ruled by her emotions. She is a challenge to suppress."

"Let her rest, then. I will watch over her and heal her."

"She is in your capable hands. I will see you again soon, Dione."

"They call me Cleo during this time in history."

"Cleo, then. I will fade for now but make no mistake that I am here and I will soon emerge."

"I have no doubts." Cleo kissed her once again as Nemesis faded within Carmen.

"Okay, you have been acting so weird since you came back from the museum." Kendall dipped a french fry in ketchup and made lazy circles. "You're not even eating your fries and fingers. They're your favorite."

Lefty's Fries and Chicken Fingers was their favorite hangout. It always had been since Kendall's mother opened it when he was nine. His father had been laid-off and they used their retirement money to open the small storefront restaurant to sell her specialty. Everyone raved about them, and the place took off like a rocket. There were now three *Lefty's* around the city and two food trucks in rotation.

"Dr. Fletcher was acting so bizarre today." PJ had not even touched her chicken. "He had me cataloging a box of stuff that came in. He went away to check on something, then came back."

"Oooh, that is soooo eerie." Kendall rolled his eyes.

"Stop it," PJ wasn't in the mood for her friend's sarcasm. "I'm being serious. He saw me looking at a ceremonial knife, then he looked at it. He said there were hieroglyphs that were rare and out of place. Then he just took the whole box from me and ran off down the hall to another room."

"Flaking out isn't strange behavior, gurl." Kendall ate a fry.

"It is when the person flaking out has never flaked in their life before."

"You don't know that. I swear if you weren't a lesbian, I would think you were in love with him."

PJ cracked a smile, "I suppose he would probably be my type."

"So, what do you think it said—the little petroglyph."

"Hieroglyph, dork. A petroglyph is a cave painting."

"Whatever, you know what I mean."

"I have no idea what it meant, but it meant something to him. He actually took the whole box with him."

"You said that. Into a secret room."

PJ sighed, ignoring Kendall. "I want to know what freaked him out."

"Why don't you just go into that room and look for yourself."

"I can't just go in there."

"You have a badge. You're there all the time. Why can't you?" grinned Kendall. "You scared? Come on, I'll go with you."

"I don't want to piss off Dr. Fletcher."

"Oh, come on. Your boyfriend won't mind. He won't even find out."

"He's not my boyfriend." PJ held up a plastic fork. "Don't make me stab you in the eye."

The two of them hopped in PJ's very late-model Ranger pickup and were downtown a half hour later. PJ could park for free in the employee structure because of her intern status. The security personnel at the employee entrance were familiar with her and greeted her warmly. They didn't seem to mind that she had another teen in tow with her.

"So where is this secret office?" Kendall asked as their footsteps echoed in the voluminous museum.

"Why don't you say it a little louder? I don't think they heard you in Chicago."

"Oh, come on, really?"

She stopped him. "It's a museum. Your voice travels. You never know who may hear us."

"What would they hear? My fabulousness?"

"I don't know. Maybe they would be super suspicious of us." She poked him in the chest. "I don't want you messing this up for me. I can't believe I let you talk me into coming down here."

"I didn't talk you into anything. You know you wanted to come."

She sighed. "Why do I ever listen to you?"

"Because you love me. Let's go. You don't want to be caught lingering by the Van Gogh on the security cameras."

"There are no Van Goghs here." She sighed.

They began to walk again. The hallways were like a maze for Kendall, but PJ seemed to know her way like a rat who had already found the cheese. Then they rounded a corner and were in the Egyptian area where caution tape warned of construction. There were toolboxes, drywall, tiling equipment, and various other things for building and exhibit.

"What's this all about?" Kendall asked as they passed it.

"New exhibit about Isis."

"The terrorists?"

"No, the goddess. Really?"

"I was serious. I don't know about this old stuff."

PJ ignored him. She pulled out her ID card and opened the security lock on the office door. Inside it was dark and it smelled of old things. She turned on the lights, and above them the fluorescents popped and hummed to life.

"Creepy." Kendall ran a finger through some dust on an old metal bowl. "Don't you ever dust?"

"Please don't touch anything."

"Sorry, is that sacred dust or something?"

"It could be."

"Is this the secret room? If it is, it's a really bad secret."

"No, it isn't the secret room. I wanted to make sure no one was in here." She walked over to another desk. "I also wanted to see if there was a key or something I could have missed. I can't really look around with Dr. Fletcher in here with me."

"If it is a secret room, do you really think he would leave a key sitting around? He doesn't seem that dumb to me."

PJ threw up her hands. "You're right. He wouldn't do that. I have no idea how we could get in."

"Let's look at it first and see. Maybe it'll be loose, maybe it isn't even locked."

PJ agreed. The two of them stepped back into the hall. Satisfied that it was clear, PJ led Kendall to the door into which Dr. Fletcher took the mysterious artifacts. Kendall grabbed the knob and it was securely locked.

"See I told you it was locked. Come on, let's go before someone finds us."

"Hold on," said Kendall. "Did you notice this door doesn't have one of those badge security thingies?" Then his eyes brightened. "I have an idea! Wait here."

"No, Kendall..." he disappeared down the hall. "This is not going to end well."

In no time, he returned with a hammer and flat-head screwdriver. "I knew they'd have tools in that construction stuff."

"Wait, what are you gonna do?" She blocked him from approaching the door. "You aren't going to break the window or lock, are you?"

"No, I'm not going to damage anything." He eased her aside. "Trust me. I used to break into my brother's room like this. He never knew a thing." Kendall approached the door and raised the hammer and screwdriver.

"I don't think we should..." PJ grabbed the hammer.

"Dr. Fletcher will kill me."

Kendall pulled at the hammer, but her grip was strong. "Let go of the hammer, PJ."

"No," she resisted even more.

Kendall pulled harder, "You don't have to prove your superior upper body strength, so let it go." He yanked the hammer. "Come on!"

Suddenly her grip vaporized, and the hammer snapped. Instead of just being freed from PJ's grip the metal of the head smashed the window of the door.

"Oh shit!" He dropped the hammer.

"Holy crap, Kendall! What did you do?"

"I didn't do it, you did it! You wouldn't let go."

"Come on! We gotta get out of here."

Kendall grabbed her hand. "Wait. Look." He pointed at the window. "WTF?"

The glass didn't shatter completely, but a spider web of cracks stretched from the impact point. But…they were closing, as if the cracks were healing. Each little crack resealed, and where a shard fell out—new glass formed.

"Did you see that?" PJ reached out to touch the glass that was now solid and untouched.

"I am seriously freaked out right now." Kendall still had the hammer and screwdriver in hand. "I gotta see that again." He smacked the window again and it shattered.

"Kendall!" It was too late to stop him.

Like the first time, though; the glass healed itself.

"I don't understand…" said Kendall. "I definitely want to see what's in there now."

"We are leaving." PJ put her hand on the knob, "Don't touch the door. Let's go."

"You want to see what's in there as much as I do." Kendall looked over his shoulder, "Someone's gonna come soon. Do you want to help me or not? If not, just go out to your truck and I will meet you."

"I hate when you do this to me, make me an accomplice against my will." PJ stepped away.

Kendall turned to the door, located the heavy hinges, and used the screwdriver and hammer to knock the pins out. They were old and laden with layers of paint. The paint split as the pins were tapped out of the hinges. In quick succession, Kendall had the three hinge pins removed. PJ helped him pull the door free from the jamb and the set it along the wall.

"Five minutes," she said. "Got it?"

Kendall put the pins in his pocket, "Got it."

Together they stood in front of the opening and looked upon an empty room. PJ was so confused. Surely, Dr. Fletcher brought the box of artifacts into this room. She saw it with her own eyes. This was the correct door.

"I don't understand," she said.

"It's an empty room. All that for an empty room?" He stepped across the threshold. "I'm still going in. Something funky is happening here."

It was a room with no windows but appeared to be an old lab classroom. There also were no other doors. The old wooden floor was scratched and scarred. Low along the walls, just above the trim, were cast iron radiators.

PJ was just as confounded as Kendall. "I don't get it."

"What's not to get? There is nothing here."

"But I saw Dr. Fletcher come in here. No doors. No windows. Nothing."

"Maybe he was in here but left later, and you didn't see him." Kendall stepped back out and looked down the hall. "We can't stay in here forever. There's nothing here. Come on, let's go."

PJ was so focused on the emptiness that she didn't hear him. "I just don't get it…"

Kendall grabbed her by the arm. "You'll get something if we don't get out of here. Come on, help me put the door back on."

Together, they put the heavy door back on the hinges and

secured it with the pins. Kendall checked it to see if it closed properly, and once it did, he could not get it to open again. Somehow it re-locked as if it was untouched.

EPIS☉DE THREE

Ray

Ray couldn't get a song out of his head as he trained with the football team in the heat and humidity.

Man, it's a hot one. Like seven inches from the mid-day sun.

It wasn't even 9:15 a.m. and it was burning hot. All the guys were struggling with wind sprints. However, they had no choice. They wanted to repeat as conference champions in the fall, and maybe win the state championship this year.

"Wake up, Kellan!" The coach called him out by name. "You daydreaming?"

Ray shook the sweat out of his eyes and focused. He was playing fullback this year. He had gotten too heavy and muscular to be quick enough for wideout—his usual position. Ray didn't care, he was looking forward to stepping back from the spotlight. The possibility of accidentally hurting someone was too great now. He was even more indestructible as he put on more mass.

"Okay, ladies!" yelled the coach. "Two laps then hit the showers. This afternoon we'll work on special teams." They all began to head out. "Ray Kellan! Come over here for a minute."

Fuck, was all Ray could think. Why was he calling him out? The heat was killing him already, so Ray stripped off his soaked practice shirt. Then, he jogged to the coach and they walked together.

"You wanted to see me, Coach?"

"I wanted to tell you I'm impressed with how big you're getting. You're gonna be great at fullback."

"Thanks, Coach."

"So…" he hesitated. "Are you juicing?"

Ray was taken by surprise. "No, I'd never do that." The coach didn't know it was physically impossible for Ray to take steroids, because his skin was impervious to needles. "I couldn't if I wanted to."

Coach laughed. "Scared of needles?"

"No, it's wrong."

"That's not what I wanted to talk to you about, anyway. I want you to start working with Sanchez and Marcos. They've got a lot of potential at your old position, but they're only sophomores. I'm making them your project."

"Sure, Coach. No problem."

"Glad to hear it," smiled the coach. "Now get yourself cleaned up or you'll be late for class."

The coach stopped and let everyone go on ahead. He took out his phone and looked at his text messages. He selected a thread from *DrFletch* and began typing out a message. Meanwhile, Ray caught up to the two sophomores who were walking together.

"Sanchez. Marcos. Wait up!" said Kellan. The underclassmen halted. "Coach wants us to start working on the wideout position. That's a good sign. You may get to start in the fall."

They all walked together into the locker room. Football,

football, football—that was the obsession. Ray welcomed that focus. He didn't want to think about his summer, and the way his body had changed. It wasn't the gains and the muscle; it was the imperviousness. He was so worried about hurting someone if they ran into him, especially on the field, and he didn't want to quit the team. He loved his team. It was his family.

As they exited the locker room after getting ready, Ray offered to sit with the guys at lunch. They were more than happy to have a school superstar sit with them. It would totally raise their game in every sense of the word.

Ray went to his locker and removed his books for first period Calc. He dug out his notebook and hoped to get a quick look at his homework. Ray hated math, but apparently, he was good at it. He knew what everyone thought about him at school: blessed with looks, athletic ability, brains. But if they only knew how insecure he was. Ray walked on egg shells. No one could know that he could put his hand through a glass window without a cut, or have a car hit him and walk away unscathed, while the vehicle suffered front-end damage. Both were events from the past summer that he prayed no one found out about. It took all his charm to convince the woman who hit him to leave him alone. He didn't need an ambulance. He wasn't hurt. He didn't even move an inch off his position when she hit him going 40 miles per hour.

"Mr. Kellan," he heard the voice of Dr. Andrews, the counselor, from behind.

Ray shut the locker. "Hey, Dr. Andrews." He noticed the counselor was not alone. There was a very attractive girl with red hair and green eyes standing with him.

"This is Calliope Garner. Just moved here from Chicago."

"Hey," she said, averting her eyes from direct contact with Ray.

"Hey," replied Ray.

"Wow, that is quite the level of sophisticated communication," said Dr. Andrews sarcastically. "Mr. Kellan, Ms. Garner's locker is right next to yours. I thought you'd be a great ambassador to our new student here at McCammon High."

Calliope wanted to die. *My first day and I have the hottest dude on the planet babysitting me. Kill me now.* "Sorry."

Ray smiled, "Don't worry about it. Seems like I'm the go-to Boy Scout leader today."

"Are you a Boy Scout?" Calliope smiled.

"Maybe…" It was Ray's turn to avoid eye contact and blush. He looked down at her book. "Looks like we have the same first period."

"I'm telling you something is totally messed up at that museum," Kendall munched on a french fry at *Lefty's.* "You're nuts if you go back there."

"Will you relax," said PJ. "There has to be an explanation. It was some kind of security system that we don't know about. Probably all the museums and galleries have shit like that to protect valuable stuff."

"It wasn't a security system. The window *healed* itself, dear. We both saw it."

"I still think it some kind of advanced security system."

"You keep thinking that," said Kendall. "With all that old crap coming in from around the world, it's probably some kind of curse or trapped demon."

"Now you're being ridiculous." PJ hesitated. "I got to admit it was really strange."

"It gave me the creeps. I am never going back there with you again."

PJ wasn't really listening to Kendall anymore. "Things got weird after we got that box of artifacts from Egypt."

"See, I'm right. Cursed artifacts. You touched it. You probably started the ball rolling on the death of humanity. You've probably got ancient Coronavirus." Just then, Kendall's mother poked her head out of the door and addressed her son.

"What mom? We're in an important conversation."

"Well you can continue your important conversation as you drive to the other restaurant on Gratiot. They're out of potatoes and the shipment doesn't come until tomorrow. I need you to take two 50-pound bags over there."

Kendall rolled his eyes. "I can't carry those."

"You have done it before. Now, get going. They're almost out and the counter is busy."

Kendall stood. "Do you want to go with me?" He poked at a distracted PJ. "Hey, did you hear me?"

"What?" she shook herself back to reality.

"I have to take some potatoes over to the other store. Do you want to go with me?"

"No," she declined. "I have some things to do at home for school."

"Like what? We're inseparable." Then, his eyes lit up. "Ah, you are gonna back to the museum to do something stupid?"

PJ gave him a slap. "Shut up. You think you know me."

"I do, my love." Kendall gave her a kiss on the cheek. "Call me later if you aren't dead, okay?"

"I won't be dead."

PJ gathered her things and began to walk home. Kendall tended to his task and loaded up the potato sacks into the customized *Kia Soul* with *Lefty's* emblazoned in screaming graphics all over the vehicle. He dreaded being seen in that. Why couldn't they have a business *Maserati* or *Land Rover*?

It didn't matter, though. He just wanted to get it done. Kendall pulled out into traffic, streamed Spotify on the radio, and set off across town. As he drove and sang loudly, he noticed a dark SUV behind him. He didn't know why this bothered him, but it just wasn't right, thought Kendall. He turned left down a side road off his normal path. The SUV did the same.

"Fuck," said Kendall.

He took another turn further off his path. The vehicle ghosted his move. Then, it sped up. The SUV was getting close to his rear bumper. Kendall disconnected his phone from the radio and called PJ. He went faster, and so did the other vehicle.

"Hello?" answered PJ.

"OMG, someone is following me."

"What are you talking about?"

Kendall looked in the rearview mirror. "A dark SUV has been following me since I left the restaurant."

"No one is following you," sighed PJ. "Drama queen."

"Oh, fuck!" Kendall shouted as the SUV bumped the rear of his Kia. "He just ran into me!"

"Seriously?" PJ was now genuinely concerned. "Drive to a police station or someplace really public."

The vehicle backed off again. Adrenaline flooded Kendall's blood. Nerves alive, sweat soaking his back and underwear. "Fuck. Fuck. I am shitting myself. What is going on?"

Then, from behind the SUV, there was the loud obnoxious roar of a powerful motorcycle. Kendall looked in the rearview mirror. Indeed, a crotch rocket street bike was speeding up alongside the SUV. The rider had a dark helmet, dark leather jacket, and a gun in his hand. He pointed it at the SUV driver's window.

Suddenly, the SUV peeled off down a side street and the motorcycle followed. Kendall pulled off to the side and parked the vehicle. He was soaked with sweat and his hands were like vice grips on the steering wheel.

"Jesus," he whispered.

"Kendall!" He could hear PJ yelling in the phone sitting on the passenger seat. "What is going on?"

He picked up the phone. "You will not believe this. I need to call the police."

"What happened?"

"A motorcycle came up alongside the SUV and pointed a fucking gun at the driver!" Kendall wiped his face with his shirt. "What the hell is going on?"

"Listen, just come over here. Finish what you have to do and come over. We'll figure out what to do."

"Okay, okay," agreed Kendall. "You have weed? I need some weed."

"Yes, I do."

Jesse Nash stormed through the tattoo shop door. There were no customers, and that was good. He was agitated and aggressive. He put his motorcycle helmet on the counter and took off his heavy leather jacket. Cleo was sitting on the couch, playing on her phone.

"What's up?" she asked.

"The *Wire*, that's what's up. The *Wire* is here. I just scared them off one of those stupid teenagers Fletcher has working for him at the museum."

"Jesus, really?" Cleo put the phone down and paid attention.

"I was checking them out, because they go to the high school where Ray Kellan is at. It seemed a little coincidental."

"You don't trust him, do you?"

"I don't know, Cleo," replied Nash. "He used to be *Wire* himself at one point. Professor Fletcher has an interesting past that could compromise someone with less integrity."

"That was a complicated arrangement, to say the least." Cleo went to him. She rubbed her hands down his tattooed, muscular arm. "No one really knows the truth, do they? It's all speculation as far as anyone is concerned. People talk and spread rumors to discredit the people we have trust in. The truth may be unknowable in this case."

He looked down into her bright, azure eyes. "He knows." Nash changed the subject. "So, how is the girl? Has she woken up yet?"

Cleo shook her head. "No. She went through a hell of an experience. She may sleep for days."

There was a troubled expression on Nash's face. "Doesn't anyone miss her? Does she have family? Another mystery with Fletcher."

"I can't read her very well. She is a strong girl, and my telepathy can't get in."

"Well, at least she has some privacy from all of us. How much do you think she knows about all of this?"

"Who knows?" replied Cleo. "Dr. Fletcher is the only one who has talked to her. We only got her when she was comatose."

"Typical," groused Nash.

"How is the kid in school?"

"Ray?" asked Nash, a little color blushing in his face.

"No, Calliope."

"She is in there. That's all I know. All our people have eyes on them both. Things are quiet."

"But now the Wire is in town, and that bothers you?"

"It should bother all of us. Those bastards are cruel."

"Why are they so interested in Ray?"

"Because everyone seems to think he is more than just *earthborne*. At least they do."

"I haven't heard that from the oracles."

"I have heard it from folks more on the fringe. There is buzz that there is more to this kid, and the Wire wants to eliminate him just to be sure he doesn't cause any uprisings, or something like that."

"So just kill him to be safe?"

"Basically," replied Nash.

"That is messed up. Killing an innocent kid to keep the peace."

Nash smoothed his dark beard out of habit when he thought. "There are so many things in play it is making me nervous." He stopped as a distant moan came from the other room. "I think she's awake."

They went into the room, and indeed Carmen was stirring. Cleo knelt down and comforted her. Nash fetched a bottle of water from a small nearby fridge.

"Hey, hey," soothed Cleo as she stroked the girl's hair. "It's okay. You're safe."

Panicked, Carmen struggled to sit up, her blind eyes wide

open. "Where am I? What's going on?"

"Here, take this." Nash put the cold bottle in her hand. "It's water."

Carmen opened the top and tossed it aside. "Thank you." She guzzled it. "Where am I?"

"You're in my tattoo shop," Nash also knelt to Carmen. "You're safe."

"Where's Professor Fletcher?"

"He isn't here right now," answered Cleo.

"Who are you people?" Carmen was trying to get up, but Nash put a strong hand on her shoulder. "How many people are here?"

"Take it easy. You have been through a lot in the last few days. You need to rest."

"You're with friends," added Cleo.

Carmen relaxed. "I need to talk to the professor."

Nash shared a glance with Cleo. "We're his colleagues. I'm Cleo, and he's Jesse. Do you want to tell us? Maybe we can help you. Is it about your time in the Veil?"

"You know about the Veil?" asked Carmen.

Cleo sighed. "Unfortunately, the Veil is something everyone knows about whether they know it or not. Even ordinary folks."

"I'm not ordinary," commented Carmen.

"That we know." Nash tried a different tact. "I am Fletcher's assistant. Do you want me to reach out to him with a message?"

"Will he come faster?" Carmen's eyes darted, unfocused. "I have to tell him what I saw—what happened to me in there."

"What did happen?" prodded Nash.

Carmen hesitated. Exhaustion crept upon her body. Cleo reached out and took her hand. Although she meant to comfort the girl, she also searched her mind. The complex barriers that were present when she was unconscious were now gauzy, opaque. Feelings swirled but were undefined and distant. However, Cleo recognized the presence of Nemesis.

"Just rest for now," Cleo let go of her hand.

"Okay," relented Carmen. "I won't fight it."
Nash and Cleo shared yet another knowing glance.

EPIS●DE FOUR

There's a Big Bad Fucking World Out There

"Did you watch the video?" asked Kendall over the phone.

"Yes. For the one millionth time, yes."

"Well?"

"Well it is fucked up," replied PJ. "I don't know what to tell you about it. I think someone was trying to carjack you or rob you."

"Carjack my mom's restaurant car? I don't think so. It has giant pictures of chicken fingers and fries on it, remember?"

PJ was in her room. She got up and went to the window as Kendall rambled on. She half-listened to his conspiracy theories, and his insistence that it was linked to the weird glass window that could repair itself. She parted the curtains and looked out into the gloaming. Across the street, in the stand of thick trees, PJ thought she saw a figure.

"There's someone across the street," said PJ as Kendall

continued his desultory rambling. "Can you shut up for a minute?"

"What?"

"I said that there is someone standing in the trees across the street."

There was a momentary pause. "No way. I know you, don't do anything stupid. Call the police or something."

PJ turned off the lights and went back to the curtain and parted it as inconspicuously as she could. There was a dark figure, but it was more like a shape. It had moved slightly closer to one of the large oak tree trunks. The other foliage and shadows still shrouded it, though.

"I'm not sure," confessed PJ. "I think you've got me freaked out. I'm seeing things. I think there's just a shadow or something."

"Can you take a picture?"

"It's too dark," replied PJ. "I think I'll take Riley for a walk."

"What's he gonna do? He's afraid of his own shadow."

"He's a pitbull. He can be intimidating."

Kendall sighed, "Oh, please. He is not."

"It's nothing, I'm sure of it. I have to take him out anyway. I'll call you later and fill you in."

"Unless you're dead."

"Stop," sighed PJ. Then she hung up, "God, he is such drama queen."

PJ put on her sneakers and *University of Michigan* ballcap. Downstairs, her brown pitbull jumped around her anticipating what was coming. He knew it was time to go out. PJ considered her dog. He was a beast and was built like a bodybuilder. But Kendall was right, he was a total puss.

"Okay, let's go." She fixed his leash to his collar.

The sultry night promised rain. Insects sang, and the twinkling of fireflies was a Tiffany necklace in the tree-line. Riley tugged at his leash, urging PJ to move faster. He had business. They began walking towards the road, and PJ carefully scanning the trees where she saw the figure. There was nothing now. She probably imagined it. Riley pulled harder.

Kendall had a way of working her up, getting her to panic and be too emotional just like him. Still, he was her best friend and knew all of her secrets. Riley led them down the road. There was a white ranch-style fence separating the thick trees from the road. Luckily, the city frequently sprayed for mosquitoes but there were a few out buzzing around. She swatted one on Riley's rear end, leaving a splatter of blood. The dog stopped, the hair on his back rose in a line down to his tail.

"I'm sorry, Riley." PJ patted him. "Was that too hard?"

But it wasn't the swat that disturbed the dog. He growled and peered off into the darkness. The growls were not his usual if he saw a squirrel or a cat, they were guttural and terrifying. He gave a few deep barks and pulled hard at the leash.

"Riley, calm down boy." PJ looked ahead. "There's nothing out there."

Suddenly, he jerked forward with all his pitbull muscle, and PJ lost control of the leash. In a fury of growls and barks, Riley ran off into the darkness. PJ's stomach sank. He was gone. He was out there. If there was someone in the darkness, her only protection had abandoned her. She took out her phone and dialed.

"Hello?" answered Kendall after a few rings.

"Riley's gone. He just ran off into the dark. He was growling and barking like I've never seen him."

"Hold on, you're talking too fast."

"Okay, listen. I took Riley out for a walk and we…"

Kendall finished the sentence, "…and you went out look-ing for the man in the shadows across the street. PJ, I told you what happened to me. It's probably the same guy. I'm telling you something is really wrong, and it all has to do with Dr. Fletcher."

"You don't know that."

"Yes, I do. You know my feelings are never wrong. When I know…*I know!*"

"What should I do?"

"Go home and call the police."

"What will they do? Nothing," PJ scoffed. "Nothing happened. There is no crime. I wasn't attacked. My dog just ran away." She didn't give Kendall time to protest, "I'm going to look for him."

"Bad idea," said Kendall. "Have you seen any horror movies—*ever*? You're a murder victim waiting to happen."

"OMG, shut up. I will call you later." PJ disconnected and shoved the phone in her pocket.

PJ was only momentarily scared; she was more concerned with the safety of Riley. It was still light enough to see shadows and shapes. The sodium street lights were quite a distance apart, allowing for deep pools of shadows to form. PJ took a deep breath to call for her dog, but then hesitated. If someone were out there, calling for Riley would surely tip them off. However, as she ruminated further, if someone was watching her, they already knew exactly where she was.

She took her keys from her pocket and nestled one between the fingers of her clenched fist. If she were going down, someone would have a nasty scar by which to remember her. PJ centered herself on the blacktop road that had a dashed yellow line down the middle. Each side had a deep ditch, and the driveways to the houses were far apart. In the haze of the sickly yellow streetlamps, bats fed on the bugs swarming them.

"Riley!" She decided to call for her dog. "Here boy!" PJ began walking down the center, keeping alert for cars or strangers. "Riley! Come on, boy!"

She progressed, calling for Riley. Sweat ran down her back, under her breasts, and pooled in her fist that was tightly clenched around the keys. Usually, there was a car or two. But not tonight. It was desolate. The road had a large rolling hill, and PJ was at the bottom of it. There were no houses on either side, and the trees were oppressive hands reaching out for her.

Then, the light caught the silhouette standing at the top of the hill. Imposing and dark, the figure started to walk down the middle of the road. A man. PJ stopped in her tracks and immediately reversed herself. She was jogging away, but he matched her pace. PJ ran. She ran hard, but he was gaining on her.

"Help me!" cried PJ. "Someone!"

She turned to look back to see where he was and tripped on the pavement. The raw blacktop tore her flesh, embedding tiny pebbles in her fresh wound. PJ scrambled to get to her feet, but he was on her. She turned to face him, keys still in her fist. He stood over her, but he didn't have a chance to attack. For from behind him, another shadowy figure intercepted his assault. There were two new figures, not just one.

"Now, it's time to learn." It was Fletcher's voice.

"Professor?" cried PJ.

"Stay down!" he ordered. Then he turned to his companion, "Your turn."

The second shadowy figure struck out with a flurry of kicks and punches. The original attacker easily blocked the blows and returned some of his own. Then they got down to it: fists, kicks, blood, teeth. It was difficult for PJ to understand what she was watching. The two combatants were moving so fast and fighting so hard she couldn't tell them apart. Then, one struck a blow to the other's chest and he was face down on the pavement. The dominant fighter pulled at the watch on his hand and spooled out a shiny piece of wire that glinted in the streetlights.

He didn't have a chance to attack the fallen man, though. Fletcher also pulled a strand of shiny wire out of his aperture and wrapped it around the man's neck. Pulling with his might, the twisted wire cut the man's throat and he buckled to the pavement.

"I had him!" said Nash angrily as he got up off the black top. "You didn't have to do that."

"He had you," Fletcher let the wire retract back into the aperture. He turned to PJ, "Are you hurt?" She just dumbly shook her head. "Good." He helped her up, then handed her a piece of candy. "I want you to chew on this. It will help with the pain."

"Huh?" She looked down at her bleeding knees. "Oh, yeah."

Fletcher returned his attention to Nash. "I owe you an apology. The Wire is in town already. Faster than I expected."

"I'm still pissed that you killed him," Nash kicked the corpse. "I needed that training."

"I'm afraid you are going to get plenty of training in the near future."

"Professor, what's going on?" PJ was regaining her place in reality. "Did you kill that guy?"

"Yes, I killed him."

PJ started to panic; her stomach heaved. "Oh, my God. That's a dead guy! That's a dead guy! I'm going to jail. Oh this is horrible."

He took her by the shoulders. "Calm down, and breathe deeply. The medicine I gave you will help. Do you feel it relaxing you?"

She took a deep breath and exhaled. "Yeah, I do feel a little calmer." Her head swam and the night took on a surreal water-color texture. "I am feeling really weird."

Nash stood next to them. "Memory elixir?"

Fletcher nodded. "She won't remember a thing."

"I'll take care of the body, and you get her back home." Nash whistled and Riley came bounding out of the darkness. "Can I keep him? She won't remember him coming back."

"Sure," Fletcher hoisted the now unconscious PJ over his shoulder. "But if she does remember, you have to give him back."

Ray was eating lunch in the cafeteria when he saw Calliope enter. She was speaking casually with two of the more popular girls in school, Rachel and Monica Smith, who were twins. Calliope scanned the lunch room and saw Ray sitting alone. She gave a quick good-bye to the twins and came over.

"Hi," said Ray.

"Hey," Calliope sat down next to him at the table. "How does a guy like you sit alone for lunch?"

He laughed. "I'm not that kind of guy, I suppose." He gestured towards Rachel and Monica, "I see you've made new friends."

"Yeah, they seem nice."

"Ever seen *Mean Girls*...?" Ray let the question trail off.

Calliope grinned. "Really? Those two?"

He nodded, "Two of the worst in the school." He took a deep drink of milk from one of five containers on his tray.

"That's a lot of milk."

"Fantastic source of protein," he replied. "I gotta keep my size if I want to earn a scholarship. It's the only way I'm going to college."

"You're amazing," she said. "And besides, I bet your parents wouldn't let you miss college. Smart and handsome."

He blushed. "I just have my mom."

"Sorry, I didn't mean anything."

"No worries. Do you miss Chicago? I bet it is a lot slower around here than you're used to."

"It's only been a few weeks," she said. "I haven't really had time to really process the difference."

"Why did your family come here? Work?"

Calliope hesitated with her answer. "Kind of. My dad did get a better job, but...I was going to be kicked out of my school."

"For what?"

"I have a little anger problem."

Kellan laughed. "You? You seem like a calm person to me. Are you like Bruce Banner, or something?"

"Yeah, something like that." She changed the subject. "So, what is there to do around here?"

"Not much," he replied. "What kind of things do you like to do?"

"I like to shop."

"Ugh, I hate shopping. The twins are good for that, though."

"I also like running."

His eyes lit up, "I'm always up for a good run."

"Very cool."

"Well, if you're up for it I'm going for a run after practice. There is a really awesome trail that runs along the river. Delaney Park."

"You're going after practice? Won't you be tired?"

"Yeah, but I love it. It clears my head."

"You must have a lot going on in there," she gave his head a playful tap.

"Unfortunately, there is." He sighed. "So, you want to come?"

"I'll have to go home and get changed, but I'm up for it. I have your number and I'll text you if I can't come. Fair?"

"Totally." He put up his fist for a bump. "It's easy to find. It's at the end of Delaney Road."

Calliope looked at him like he was crazy, then bumped his fist with hers. "You're on, handsome."

Nash looked at his phone. He was waiting for a text message from Fletcher. He'd been silent for too many hours and it made him nervous. He'd just finished with a client who was getting a sleeve of hipster tribal art. Nash thought it was ridiculous, but he didn't mind taking the guy's money. He preferred doing artwork that meant something to a person.

"Hey."

Startled, Nash looked up to see Carmen awake. "Feeling better?"

"Yeah," she replied. "I'm getting my balance and my strength back."

"You hungry?" He put the phone down on the counter. "There's a Coney Island across the street. It's good."

She nodded. "Just something light, thanks. I don't know if I can keep it down."

He laughed. "I get it. If you want to watch TV or something I can turn it on." He pointed to a small Samsung mounted over his studio area. "I don't like it on, but when I have a client in the chair for a few hours it keeps me from having to listen to them. They think I'm a fucking therapist sometimes."

He saw her struggle momentarily, feeling for her way in the room, and then felt stupid. "God, I'm sorry. I'm a dumbass." Nash went over and helped her to the leather sofa flanked with tables heaping with tattoo magazines.

"Thanks, I'm usually pretty good at getting around." Carmen hesitated. "You know my story, right?"

"Yeah, I do. And what you went through would take away anyone's bearings for a long time." He picked up his phone again. "You like an omelet?"

"Ham, cheese, and mushroom."

"Coffee?"

"Yes, please."

He went to the door. "I'll go get it." He opened it, but before he stepped through, he paused. "Do me a favor, I'm putting up the closed sign. Don't let anyone in."

She nodded. "Where is Cleo?"

"She went out somewhere, I don't know."

"Oh, I thought you two were…"

He laughed. "No, we're not. She's more like a baby sister to me even though she's the older one. Older by *a lot*." Then, he left.

She wondered what that meant but dismissed it. Carmen didn't have the energy to think about anything deep or cryptic. All she wanted was food, and to sleep for three more days. She walked over to the sofa and sprawled haphazardly upon it. It was soft, and there were pillows. Putting one under her neck, Carmen relaxed. Luckily, the way was clear and there wasn't anything to trip on. Did Nash expect her to watch TV, or did he not remember she was nearly totally blind? Maybe, he meant just listen to it. Either way, he didn't tell her where the remote was even if she wanted to.

The silence was a blessing. Her mind was so noisy with all sorts of images and static. There were memories trying desperately to be remembered, and others struggling to fade away. Ghosts from the Veil were in there, too. Then there was a commotion outside the front door. It was too soon for Nash to be back from the restaurant. There was a key turning in the door.

Carmen sat up. Her instincts to fight ignited. Anything could be a weapon for her. In her veins her connection to the Veil stirred. The remnants of the visit were like electricity, a certain high that opened her mind to colors, smell, and sounds. Ribbons of energy turned and swelled. Her eyes took on a silvery, moon-lit iridescence, and she could "see" the room with her remaining senses. The door had been unlocked, and it was opening much more slowly than expected.

"*Help me.*"

It was Cleo, whispering. Then, there was a muffled thud as she fell through the threshold. Carmen was up like a bolt, and she used her senses to navigate to her. She could sense something was terribly wrong.

"Oh my God! Cleo?"

"Yes, please. Where's Jesse? It's happening. I need him."

Carmen was able to make it to her. "He will be back in just a second. I promise. Let me help you to the couch."

Cleo pulled herself up using Carmen's body. "No, I need to get in the chair."

"I can't see, you'll have to guide us." She propped Cleo's arm over her shoulder. "Where is it?"

"Like ten feet." She led them. "You're doing it."

They made it to the tattooing chair, which was set up for a customer to receive a back tattoo. Cleo fell forward into it, allowing her knees to nearly touch the floor. Carmen had to guess if she was in a good position.

"Are you okay? Is there something I can do?"

"No, thank you." Cleo sighed. "I will be okay. I just need Jesse."

As if cued, Jesse Nash walked back in. "I told you not to open the door…" He saw Cleo sprawled in the chair. "Oh, shit." He put the food on the counter and rushed over to her.

"It's happening. An omen. You need to read it." Her breath was staccato. "I haven't had one like this in two hundred years."

Gently, Nash touched Carmen to reveal his position, "You need to get back to the couch. I have to do something."

Carmen nodded and remembered the short pathway back to the couch where she sat. Her senses de-escalated as the kinetic energy in the room dissipated. Cleo's breathing was improved. Nash fetched a pair of scissors from his work table full of stainless-steel ink cups. Then, he took the hem of Cleo's T-shirt from the back and cut it open.

Her alabaster white flesh was beneath. Upon it, there were patterns of ink and color covering every millimeter. However, it wasn't a static tattoo; it was moving. Like a river, the colors flowed, the shadows thickened. Shapes and silhouettes formed and faded. Nash watched helplessly as Cleo suffered the pain of divination.

"It is still forming," said Nash.

Cleo gritted her teeth, "No shit."

"Sorry." He hated this part of divination for there was nothing he could do until the message had formed. "I can't make out anything just yet. It is moving so much."

He concentrated on the images flowing beneath the top layers of her white flesh. An image formed from the top left shoulder blade and spread crosswise and down. Dark inky clouds. A storm. Within the storm, ropey tentacles looking like slender tornadoes writhing. The tentacles connected to a great bell-shaped, cephalopod-like head. Below, two figures fighting the descending behemoth.

"Wow," gasped Nash. "I need my phone." He pulled it out of his pocket and pointed the camera at Cleo's back. "Shit!" He snapped a few pictures, "It's fading. It is fading fast."

"What?" Cleo was shocked. "The divination always stays, sometimes for years."

"Well this divination is now gone." Nash checked his phone, but the pictures were faded as well. "Your skin is clear. There's nothing now. Everything is gone."

Cleo lifted herself out of the chair, clutching the T-shirt to her breasts. She stood, twisted, and looked in the mirror. For the first time in centuries, her skin was as fresh and clear as the day she was born. At first, she was shocked. That lasted for only a second, now was a time for relief.

"No more divinations."

"For, like, ever?" asked Nash.

"I don't know," sighed Cleo. "It's a void."

Nash handed her a T-shirt advertising the tattoo shop that was on a nearby shelf. "What do you think it means?"

She slipped on the shirt, "Maybe this is the divination. Emptiness. Nothing. The world ends. Or maybe it doesn't."

The sun was burning in the afternoon sky. Indeed, Delaney Park was at the end of Delaney Road and it was easy to Google. There was a huge concrete barrier that blocked the road from the river should any runaway vehicle lose control. However, just beyond the barrier was signage denoting the running and biking trail. There were many cars in the public lot at the trailhead.

Ray was already there when Calliope found the park. He was shirtless and shiny with perspiration. Calliope was thankful she had on dark sunglasses so she could seriously check him out head to toe without looking like a pervert. Her eyes lingered on his wide shoulders, then his defined chest before going southward to hover on his abs. They were perfectly separated, lean, and reminded her of a stained-glass church window.

"Hey!" He smiled, squinting. "Glad you made it. I was getting worried that you stood me up." He fell into a stretch for his hamstrings. "I'm already sweating like a pig. Practice was brutal. Not sure how much running we will do in this heat. I don't want to get dehydrated."

Calliope held up two bottles of water. "I thought of that."

"Awesome," he took one as she approached. "It's a good trail. I think you'll like it. So how many miles do you usually do?"

Calliope was distracted by the striated muscles of his flexing shoulders. "What?"

"Miles?"

"Oh, yeah. I can probably only do three in this heat if that's okay."

"That's perfect," he replied. "The trail has markers every half mile." He slicked his wet hair back with his hands. "You need to stretch?"

"I'm good. I'll warm up. Just take it easy on me the first mile."

"You got it," he smiled. "I want to take it easy, too."

They began. Calliope kept pace with him, and Ray was considerate of her. He had been around enough lesser-in-shape people to realize she was a lot of talk. They chatted casually. Soon, though, the talk decreased as they both concentrated on breathing and stride. Calliope was easily keeping up with him, which Ray found impressive. He smiled broadly.

"What are you smiling about?" Calliope huffed, keeping her measure.

"Nothing," he replied. "Well, you."

"Me?"

Sweat dripped off his face and body. "I thought maybe you were going to be like a lot of other girls who say they want to run with me. Some of them are just saying it, and when we get out here...well..."

"So, you're testing me?" She laughed, "Am I passing?"

"Yes, you are."

"Good for me." They made the first half mile marker. "All the girls just want to hang out with you? Is that a bad thing?"

Thank God, the hot boy likes me thought Calliope. I can deal with that. The run became immensely easier.

"I don't like fake. I mean they pretend to be able to run or be into what I like, and they're really not."

"I get it," said Calliope who was now sweating as much as Ray. "But isn't it like a form of flattery?"

"I don't think so," he looked sideways at her. "I don't expect someone to like what I like just to be friends with them. People are different."

"And you think it's fake if they say they like what you like but don't really?"

"Exactly," he replied. "Probably why I don't have many close friends."

"You? Mr. Popular? I see how many people come up and talk to you." She pushed her stride to keep up with him. "You're like nice to everyone who talks to you."

"Not that many want to talk to me," said Ray. "I've been told I'm intimidating even though I try to be friendly."

"Can I be honest with you?" She didn't wait for permission and just took it. "I was totally intimidated when I was told you would be my Boy Scout. You are intimidating and it is something you won't ever solve. You are gorgeous. There I said it. The kind that intimidates people. Have you ever heard the story of the girl that was so beautiful and popular, but never had a date at all? The boys were too afraid to ask her out because she was so fierce. Everyone always thought she must have a boyfriend, but she sat home alone every Saturday because she was beautiful."

Ray laughed, "And you think that is me? Is that why I don't have many friends? I mean, I have a lot of friends at school, but they're not 'friend-friends.' Do you know what I mean?"

"I do," said Calliope, *and I bet they are all intimidated.* "I'm the same. I don't let a lot of people get close, either. They'll just hurt you. Or maybe, you're one of those people that doesn't need a lot of friends, just a few that matter. Like, I said I don't want to be burned by shitty fake people."

"...Or you burn them."

"What's that supposed to mean?" snapped Calliope. Had her stories made it to this school, too?

"Nothing." Ray was surprised she was upset. "I didn't mean you. I meant me. I don't like people getting close because I don't want anyone getting hurt."

"How would you hurt them?" She noticed the first mile marker coming up was near a picnic area. "Can we stop here?"

"Sure."

They went to the picnic table that was just off the path under a tree. It offered some sun protection, and there was a breeze coming off the river. Ray bent over and put his hands on his knees. Sweat poured off him like a faucet. Calliope sat on the edge of the seat, wiping sheets of perspiration off her face.

Momentarily, Ray caught his breath. "Why did you get so mad?"

"I thought you were implying that I hurt people."

"No, not at all. I don't even really know you well. I'd never say anything like that."

She waved her hand at him. "Don't worry about it. I was being too sensitive."

Ray sat on the bench next to her, not really sharing eye contact. "Yeah, I'm really sorry if I hurt your feelings."

She just looked at him through the safety of her sunglasses. "What is it about you?"

"What do you mean?" He looked away, avoiding eye contact.

"I mean you're are easily the nicest, and sexiest guy, I've met in a long time. But you're still like…I don't know…like guarded."

He was silent and didn't respond.

"I'm sorry," she said.

"I've only known you for two days." He looked at her. "What did you expect?"

"I don't know, I guess I expected you to be like other guys…"

"What's that supposed to mean?"

Ray's skin began to emit a faint, golden glow. He was quite

aware of it, and hoped Calliope thought it was just the reflected sunlight in his sweat.

"Don't get defensive," she continued. "I meant I totally expected you to be a jock asshole. Hit on me, or ask me out."

"Sorry to disappoint you," the glow intensified.

Calliope took off her sunglasses to look at him. "What's going on?"

"I don't know what you're talking about."

"You." She reached out to touch his hand, "You are glowing."

Ray jerked his hand back, the glow tightened around his skin like a suit of thin armor. "You're hallucinating."

"I know power when I see it," said Calliope. "You're not the only one."

He looked at her. "How would you know anything about it?"

"I got so mad because when you said I hurt people when they get close to me, because I thought you knew. Then, I thought, he *couldn't* know. He doesn't know me."

"What are you talking about?" The glow faded a little.

Calliope held up her hand, fingers spread wide. She focused on her own fingers, the slenderness of each digit, the manicured nail. Then around the knuckles, tiny balls of reddish orange light appeared. They were intense, they appeared sticky like a frog's eggs or tapioca balls. They moved towards the tips of her nails, where one popped like a firework. The thin stream of balls massed on the tips of her nails, and they too exploded with a kinetic pop.

"What was that?"

"That's the way I hurt people," said Calliope. "I can make these energy balls, or whatever they are. The 'scientists' my dad was taking me to called them plasma. More specifically, ionized plasma like in lightning, or…"

"…or like in the sun," Ray finished her sentence. "We covered it in AP Physics last year."

"People aren't supposed to be able to do that, from what I gather."

"No, I don't suppose so."

"It gets worse when I get angry, frustrated. Or jealous."

"Jealous?"

"Yeah. I have anger and jealousy issues, but I have the power to do something about it."

His eyebrows arched in surprise, "I guess so. Have you hurt anybody?"

She nodded. "I didn't mean to. I got crazy because this girl at my old school…" She paused to put the thought together, "…it's going to sound stupid. I bought these awesome Golden Goose Superstar sneakers. They cost me $1,500. Then this bitch shows up the next day with the same fucking sneakers. Everyone knew I was buying them. *I* wear Golden Goose."

"What happened?"

"I got so angry, the plasma just started pooling off my hands. I screamed at her for stabbing me in the back for buying the sneakers that she knew I was getting. Did I say that bitch was my friend?"

"Don't hang around with the twins, then."

Calliope rolled her eyes. "Anyway, I yelled at her for buying them. I pointed at them, and the plasma balls just went off my fingers like a squirt gun or fire hose. They stuck to her shoes and burned them to ash. She was burned, too."

"Oh my God. That's terrible."

"I was swooped out of that school, and we literally disappeared overnight."

"You and your family?"

She nodded. "There is a group of scientists that watch me… from a distance. They wanted to study me, but my mom and dad said no. They were there, though. Watching. They pulled some strings and got us out of there."

"My power isn't that impressive," said Ray. "I can't be hurt."

"That's amazing!" she said. "You're indestructible?"

"So far," he replied. "I survived a plane crash as a baby. The sole survivor. A car hit me going 45 this summer, and the car was destroyed."

"That glow? Is that it?"

"Yeah, want to see?" he held out his hand. "It's kind of like a Spiderman power. It activates when I don't even know it. Like seconds before something happens, it turns on to protect me. I've been starting to control it though. I've been practicing. I can push it out and make like a shell around me. And I can make smaller spheres of it around things. I put my cat in one, and he went nuts."

"That's cool."

"So, I'm like you. I don't want to hurt anyone. I can run into someone and it's like they've been hit by a brick wall. I switched positions in football because I didn't want anyone tackling me and killing themselves. I may have to quit."

"Don't quit, Ray." She said. "You can be the best player ever. Totally unstoppable."

"I'm gonna put someone in a coma or kill them. I *can't*..." He stood. "I'm getting tired. You want to call it a day and walk back?"

"Sure," she said.

"You have to promise that you won't ever tell anyone," he held her hand close. "Promise?"

Calliope's pulse raced as she looked into his blue eyes. Still, she could feel the barrier between their hands like holding a thin film of plastic, "I promise. You, too?"

"Maybe you were supposed to be here for a reason," said Ray.

"Like someone's pulling strings behind the scenes, right?" She smiled. "That sounds kind of silly."

EPIS◉DE FIVE

A New Oracle

Fletcher examined the self-repairing glass door. Even though it was a magic talisman-protected passage, there was always a flaw when it self-repaired. He ran his fingers over the small scar where it was hit with something.

Nash came up from behind. "Find something interesting?"

"Our young friends found a way to breech the glass," he said. Then he opened the door, "No matter, I expected them to try something."

"They are going to get hurt, or worse…" Nash dangled the words.

"That is why we are leaving. We are packing up and shipping out to Livonia for now."

"That's a pretty safe place, but what are you going to do about the Wire? They are here and know where to find these kids."

"I'm still thinking," said Fletcher as he handed Nash a box

full of artifacts. "Can you secure this in the car? Then come back. I think we can get the last of it in one trip."

Nash took the box and walked out of the room. Fletcher paused and scanned the assortment of artefacts remaining on the table. It was a mixture of actual, legitimate anthropological work, and a few odds supernatural pieces that still held a mystery to be revealed. But he could pursue that in the more secure environment of the Livonia establishment.

"Professor Fletcher?" He heard PJ's voice from the doorway. "What's going on? It looks like you are packing.

He looked up. "Hello, PJ. Yes, I am packing up."

"I don't understand. Are you moving labs?"

"I will be honest we have lost our funding. We have to vacate."

"Where are you going? Where are you going to put all the artifacts? What's going to happen to me? Us? My studies and getting experience?"

"The museum has storage for most of it. I will take the more valuable items with me. As for you, you are smart and will have plenty of opportunities to intern and learn far more from someone else than you can learn from me."

"This is totally unacceptable! This can't be happening. Can't you call someone?"

"Who would I call?" He wrapped some items in paper and shoved them into a box. "And what would I tell them? That a 16-year-old girl is inconvenienced and unhappy so you must reverse your decision at once."

"Sorry, I guess that was a little entitled, but you know everyone," she said.

"Indeed," he sighed. "But not the right people this time."

She watched him for many moments. Guilt was eating at her. "Is it because of me?"

"Why would it be your fault?"

"I have a confession," she said.

He stopped what he was doing and leaned on the table.

"What do you want to confess?"

"I'm sure you know…" PJ looked away from Fletcher. "…that…"

"That you tried to break in with your friend?" He shook his head, "Thank you for coming clean but I saw that on the security camera. That's not the reason."

"But we know your secret."

He stopped dead. "What do you mean? What secret do you know?"

"The window in the door. It's some kind of weird technology. It's not something we have seen before."

He sighed, relieved. "Don't worry about that. You're right, it's new security technology. It's gone now. We removed it."

"Who is 'we?'" PJ looked around, "I don't see anyone."

Just then, coming from down the hall, Jesse Nash entered. "There's enough room for the rest of these boxes. Everything else is…"

"PJ, this is my assistant Mr. Jesse Nash."

"Assistant? Since when have you had an assistant? I thought *I* was your assistant?"

Nash extended his hand, "Nice to meet you. PJ? I just got into town. I was on assignment in the field."

She apprehensively shook his hand, "Nice to meet you." PJ took in his handsome face. He was wearing a tight black T-shirt and jeans that barely contained his buff body. Kendall would go insane if he saw this man. "Where have you been? Overseas?"

"I've been in the US, but on the move a lot."

"What do you specialize in?" asked PJ.

Nash looked at Fletcher, "You're right about her, very bright and curious."

"PJ, I know there is no good time to tell you any of this, but I promise I will help you find an internship or something else to further your interest in museum work and anthropology. I'm afraid this is the end of this particular adventure in your life."

"You were just going to leave, weren't you? I happened to catch you in mid-ghost. Where are you going? You owe me that much."

Fletcher sighed. "First, I don't owe you anything. You are still a child. I don't know, but it will not be here." He returned to packing the final items that were on the table. "I probably will go back to Europe."

"Will you text me?" Tears were welling up in her eyes. "I can't believe this is happening."

Nash interrupted. "Professor Fletcher, I hate to cut this short, but we needed to be out of here ten minutes ago."

"Why?" PJ asked. "The museum wouldn't give you a hard time about packing up..." A light went on in her eyes. "...Unless you aren't supposed to take this stuff."

"It's not like that, PJ." Fletcher fit the last piece in the final box. "They want this space as soon as possible."

"That is bullshit," she said. "I don't know why you're lying to me, but I don't care."

"PJ..."

She turned to leave the room, "I don't care where you go."

Out of the room she went and hurried down the hall. Her feet echoed on the marble, masking her tears. Fuck him. PJ wanted to run, but she didn't want him to see that. It was bad enough she was crying, but she didn't want him seeing that or to think she was running from the situation. What an asshole. Good riddance. PJ hit the stairwell leading to the parking garage two levels below. She had to park in the garage instead of the surface lot because of repaving. Otherwise, she would have been in her car and out of there by now.

PJ slammed open the second level door. Even though it was a bright day, the parking garage was gloomy, dark, and poorly lit with fluorescent tubes. Water dripped unseen, but added to PJ's anxiety. The heat was stifling, like an oven. Her car was at the far end, through the shadows. Her stomach was unsettled, like the first moment going down a steep rollercoaster hill. In her mind, there was a buzz, something she was trying to remember but it fought her.

Then, in the long shadows she saw a figure. It must have been a man, for the silhouette was tall. The buzz in her brain screamed now. PJ needed to remember, but couldn't. There was a panicked alarm ripping though her chest. Sweat soaked her. Her pulse was jacked. He was not someone she needed to meet up close. PJ began to back towards the stairwell door.

"You lost?" The man asked, his voice echoing off the concrete block walls.

PJ didn't answer, she couldn't answer; her voice was paralyzed by fear. She put her hand on the handle to the stairs. His arm extended stiffly, like he was throwing something. Across the distance, a shiny wire shot out. There was a stainless-steel arrow point on it, and it stuck in the cement next to her head. Crumpling, PJ went down to her knees. He began to walk towards her. The wire retracted back to him. Closer. His steps were sure, the stride long. PJ had no weapons, no way to defend herself. And her voice would not call for help for tears were choking her now.

"Shh," he said. "No tears. I will make it quick."

He pulled the wire out from his watch and held a two-foot length of it. It shined. He wanted to make sure PJ could see it before wrapping it around her neck. However, that was his last moment. The next seconds came like a strobe light. First the lights went out completely, then a luminescent pinkish purple ribbon wrapped around his neck. Two other hands disabled his, and the wire snapped back into the watch. The ribbons pulled at his body. Anguished screams filled the parking deck. He was stretched, reaching the physical limits of his body to stay together. He gargled on his own blood. His arms separated from his torso. Then, the body dropped. The ribbons retreated into the shadows.

"Jesus Christ!" Nash shouted as he burst through the stairwell doors as the lights came back on. He located PJ and knelt by her. "Are you okay? Are you hurt?"

She just stared up at him.

"Are you hurt?" He tipped her head left and then to the right. "No cuts." He inspected the floor, "No blood." Then he turned around and saw the dismembered corpse tangled in his dark overcoat, bleeding out on the cement. Nash dialed Fletcher, "You need to come down to the second level and pick us up. Things have taken a turn." He paused to listen. "Who is us? PJ was nearly assassinated. Again."

PJ heard what he said. "What do you mean again?"

Nash silenced her with a raised hand. "Clean-up is gonna be a bitch."

No more than a half hour later, the tattoo shop door opened. Cleo was pacing and paused as she watched Fletcher and Nash enter with a teenage girl. PJ was still in shock, not really understanding what happened to her, or where she had been spirited. However, her dog Riley, who was in a back room, came bounding up to her.

"Oh, what a cute dog!" She knelt to pet him. "What's his name?"

Nash sheepishly looked at Fletcher who just sighed. "His name is Riley."

"Is he yours?" She kept rubbing his ears. "What a good boy."

"He seems to like you," Nash evaded her question.

Fletcher looked at Cleo, "Where is Carmen?"

"In the other room, why?"

"I want to introduce you both to our friend, PJ." Fletcher's eyes pierced Cleo. "Did you 'see' anything? Did you tell Carmen?"

Just then Carmen came out of the other room, "I heard my name."

"Do you know what happened in the parking garage at the museum?"

She nodded. "Don't be angry with Cleo. She had a vision and told me there was a girl in danger, I'm not about to let a female be hurt by a man if I can help it, and that it had something to do with you."

"And you…"

"…I entered the Veil and saved her life."

"That was you?" PJ stood. "I don't understand any of this but thank you so much. I need to call my parents. I need to get home."

"You'll have to stay with us for a while," said Fletcher. "It's not safe out there." He turned to Nash, "I need you to go get the boy."

He nodded, "If he's still alive." He grabbed his motorcycle helmet and left.

"If he is still alive?" PJ whirled around on Fletcher. "You're talking about Kendall, aren't you?"

"You need to calm down. You want a drink?"

"I'm underage!"

Fletcher sighed. "Oh yeah, that's right."

Carmen sat on the couch as did Cleo. "So, who was that man in the parking garage? Was it one of those 'Wire' people you talked about?"

"Yes, I'm afraid so." He went behind the counter and brought out a bottle of single malt. "I need one. Anyone else?"

"One what?" asked Carmen.

"He has whiskey," explained Cleo.

"Yeah, I'll take a shot. I need something after pulling a guy's arms off."

PJ turned to her, "That was you? How did you do that?"

"I'll tell you about it sometime," she answered, quite proud.

"I thought I was hallucinating. OMG, I am going to be sick. I saw that guy die."

"Better him than you," added Fletcher.

"He was trying to kill me?" asked PJ. "Why?"

"Because you are weak," replied Carmen.

"Hey, you don't even know me!" PJ looked at the professor, "Is this your friend?"

"Relax, she doesn't mean it in a bad way," he said. "You are young. You don't have any special abilities to speak of. You are an easy target. One obviously the Wire thinks they can use as leverage."

"Or to rattle us," said Cleo. "Make us nervous, and careless."

PJ absorbed the conversation swirling around her as if she wasn't there. Abilities? I'm weak? I have been nearly killed twice. Who the fuck were these people associating with Fletcher?

"I fell and hit my head, right? I'm in a coma. Having hallucinations." PJ looked at the people in the room. "I am making all of this up right now. Trippin' balls?"

"Trippin balls. Keep telling yourself that, princess." Fletcher slammed his whiskey.

"Come on," said PJ. "You all just said some stuff that makes no sense to me. Back it up. I am weak because I don't have abilities? What abilities?"

"I can pass through the Veil and use it," said Carmen.

"I can divine the future, and have telepathic and empathic gifts," said Cleo.

"What about you, Dr. Fletcher?" asked PJ. "Or your friend that left?"

"Jesse and I have..." he chose his words gingerly, "...experience."

PJ sighed. "This is too much. I want to go home."

"Let her go home," said Carmen.

"If she goes home now, her whole family will be in danger— probably dead before morning."

"Dead!" shouted PJ. "What kind of crap have you gotten me into? This is a nightmare."

Fletcher took out another shot glass and poured PJ a small amount. "I guess if you're old enough to die, you're old enough to have this." He took it to her. "Cheers."

Fuck it. PJ took it and slammed it down. It burned. She had never tasted hard liquor before, and at that moment didn't want to ever again. Fletcher took Carmen her shot, along with his refill, and together they downed them.

"Okay, I will tell you what you need to know."

As he was about to begin, the door opened. Jesse Nash came in with Kendall over his shoulder. Then, he put him down and removed the dark hood that had been placed over his head. Disoriented, Kendall looked around the room at the faces. They were strange, except for PJ's.

"PJ?"

"It's okay, Kendall. They won't hurt you."

He looked at Nash, "Won't hurt me? He jumped me and put a bag over my head! He said he was bringing me to you." It was then that he truly got a good look at his kidnapper: rugged, leather, beard, tattoos. "I would have come willingly," he grinned at him.

Nash sighed. "Give me one of those shots." Fletcher poured it and gave it to him. "We should not be bringing kids into this."

"You were a kid once," said Cleo. "I remember when you first came along."

"Whatever," he slammed the whiskey. "I think there was a shadowman following me."

"What's a shadowman?" asked PJ. "That guy in the garage?"

He nodded. "For want of a better word."

"And the guys that tried to run me off the road?" added Kendall.

"You're both safer here with us," said Fletcher. "Jesse, can you mark them with the cloaking rune?"

"Good idea." He walked over to the tattoo chair. "Who's first?" He took off his leather jacket, his tight T-shirt soaked and clinging with sweat. "This will be quick, and it will hide you."

Kendall grinned like a thirsty cat. "I've always wanted a tattoo. Where do you put it?"

"Take off your shirt," said Nash. Kendall smiled, and Nash just sighed and looked at PJ. "How do you even?"

PJ laughed and it felt good. "It takes a lot of effort."

"Oh, come on you people. He's beautiful," said Kendall.

"God, I'm not blind." There was an audible groan from Nash and Cleo. "What?"

Nash tapped him on the shoulder and pointed at Carmen. Then he mouthed the words *she can't see.* Kendall followed his finger and mouthed *oh shit, sorry.*

"Okay, is someone mouthing that there's a blind girl in the room?" asked Carmen. She laughed, "Fuck, don't be so obvious. And for the record, I am not totally blind. Not yet."

Kendall took off his shirt, balled it up and threw it to PJ, and got in the chair. "Will this hurt? Am I going to get addicted? Will I want to be all hot and tattooed like you?"

"If you're lucky," replied Nash as he poured black ink into a stainless-steel cup. He then fixed a small disposable needle in his gun. "Don't be nervous." With sanitary latex gloves, Nash cleaned an area of Kendall's skin. "You've got good muscle."

"Thanks," said Kendall. "So, what exactly is this tattoo?"

"It's a rune. A magical mark that will hide you from your enemies," said Cleo.

Nash was ready and turned on the power supply on the floor with his foot. The gun hummed. Then, he put the needle to Kendall's flesh. However, as he made the first line, it disappeared beneath his skin, fading away. Nash turned off the machine.

"Fletcher, Cleo," he said. "Can you come see this?" They got up and came over to the chair. PJ did so as well. "Watch." Nash made the mark again and it disappeared. "See that?"

"See what?" asked Kendall. "What's going on? Are you going to do it?"

"Did you feel that?" asked Nash. "I made two lines on your shoulder."

"I didn't feel a thing."

Fletcher looked at Cleo who was covering her mouth with her hand, disbelieving what she saw. "Can I touch you?" she asked.

Kendall nodded. Cleo lay her hands on his skin. Closing her eyes, Cleo inhaled. She took in not only air, but essence. Kendall's aura filled her. He took from her, too. Two tattoos from Cleo's fingers bled like water stains off onto his skin where they became permanent on his shoulder blades. They blended. Mixing of two souls exchanging sensations, each sharing the intimate privilege. Tears ran down his face, but not of pain or fear. They were of joy, enlightenment, satisfaction.

"Another oracle." Cleo had tears as well. She lowered her lips to the back of his neck and softly kissed him. "You are found."

"That was unexpected," commented Fletcher.

"What was that?" asked PJ. "How did her tattoos move to his body?"

"They are more runes," answered Nash. "She has given him magic. He has more protection than all of us against the Wire right now."

Cleo removed her hands and wiped her cheeks. "Kendall, are you okay?"

He pulled himself out of the tattoo chair and stood. "I feel... weird. Like I was walking in a gale on the beach, or something." He looked at his own skin, but it didn't look any different. "I feel totally weird inside."

"You have woken up," smiled Cleo. "I bet you have had premonitions all your life, right?"

He put on his shirt, "Yeah, I kind of know when things are going to happen. Or if someone is lying."

"That's a good gift to have," said Cleo. "Truth divination is rare. You will be of great service to ..." She clipped off her sentence as she got a stern glance from Fletcher.

Nash motioned for PJ to get in the chair as he changed to a new needle. "You're next."

"I don't want one," she said.

"Do you want one of the shadowmen to cut your head off with a wire?"

She gulped. "No."

"Then get in the chair," said Kendall. "It doesn't hurt."

"How do you know? Yours disappeared."

"True," he shrugged. "I still didn't feel it."

"PJ, we don't have time for this. The rune will hide you from the Wire. Or do you want to be sliced open?"

"You keep telling us about these murderers called shadow-men and the Wire, but haven't said who or what they are. Why? I feel we have a right to know." She looked at Kendall, "Right? You got my back on this?"

"Please, get in the chair," said Nash, losing his patience.

"I'll do it if you come clean. Tell us what is going on." She looked at Kendall. "And in front of him so he can tell if you're lying or not. I have a lot of questions."

Nash grinned. "Okay, now I like you. Get in the chair."

"I want it somewhere hidden. My parents will kill me."

He reached for an *Oracle Tattoo Shop* tank-top on a nearby shelf of swag. "Go put this on and come back out. The bathroom is through there." He pointed. "I'll put it on the inside of your upper arm, so close to your armpit it will look like you forgot to shave. It is that small."

PJ took the shirt and left the room.

"Is she always this difficult?" Nash asked.

Kendall nodded. Fletcher nodded, too, as he continued to dig through some of the boxes he'd brought.

"Guess you two are made for each other," said Carmen.

Kendall grinned, "Not really."

PJ came out again and sat in the chair. "Remember, no one can see this. Can you use like skintone colored ink?"

"Are your parents in the habit of inspecting your body?" said Nash sarcastically. "If they are, you got bigger problems than a tattoo."

"No," she snapped with an eye roll. "So, Dr. Fletcher, you said you would tell us everything."

"I said I'd answer your questions."

PJ winced as Nash drew a line roughly an inch long. "Okay, who are you? You're not some museum expert."

"You're wrong there, I am a museum expert."

Kendall looked at PJ. "That was the truth."

"Okay, who do you work for? Who pays your salary?"

"Good question," commented Nash as he made a few more lines.

"I don't have a salary. I have plenty of my own money."

"Then what are you doing here?" she asked, frustrated. "Have you lied to me in the last week?"

"Yes, I have lied to you."

"Truth," said Kendall.

"What about?"

"Well, the dog is really yours. Not Nash's."

"What?"

"I gave you a potion to bury your memory of last night when you were almost killed—the first time."

"The first time?" she tried to sit up.

Nash steadied her, "Almost done. You can beat him up in a minute."

"I'm not going to beat him up," said PJ.

"I would," laughed Nash. "He gave me your dog."

She huffed, "Whatever. Why did you freak out when I showed you that *Khonshu*? What is it? And don't think I forgot about the Wire shit."

"It is used in ancient rituals to make blood sacrifices."

"Gross," said Kendall.

"That answered only one question. Why did you freak out? You looked at the writing on it. What did it say?"

"It was very valuable and rare."

Kendall shook his head, "Nope."

Fletcher's muscle jumped in his jaw. "It was stolen and sent to me."

"Nope," said Kendall. "Change the question, PJ."

"Okay," she thought for a moment. "What temple or deity did it belong to?"

Nash interrupted. "All done. You didn't feel it at all." He cleaned it, "No blood either." He looked up at Fletcher and smiled, "So what's the answer, boss?"

He pointed at Nash, "You stop instigating."

"I'm enjoying this," said Carmen. "Fun to see you squirm—and hear it."

"Who did it belong to? What deity?"

"Nemesis."

"The goddess of vengeance?" asked PJ.

"More like retribution," added Cleo. "You know, doling out just desserts."

"Why did that make you freak out?"

"I'm done answering these questions." Fletcher grew angry, "This has gone from silly to irritating."

"I don't think these kids are being silly," said Nash. "Both of them have been nearly killed, and Kendall is an oracle. You should tell them what the Wire is."

"Jesse, you are my assistant. We need to have a word in private, please." Fletcher addressed the teens, "You are both safely cloaked now. You are free to go home. PJ, take your dog with you."

The room chilled.

"Wait, what about this Wire stuff?" But Fletcher was done with her.

"You seem very unsettled," observed Miss Venus as Fletcher consumed fresh cotton candy from her truck. "Sure, you don't need something stronger?"

"I probably do, to be honest." He pulled off another fluffy section and put it in his mouth. He smiled. "It's so cool how cotton candy feels melting on my tongue."

"You didn't come here to eat my candy or drink my whiskey it seems."

He thought for a moment, wondering how to open the conversation. "I guess I could ask you: did you know that the friend of PJ, my assistant at the museum, was an oracle?"

Miss Venus nodded, "I knew he was very close, but still sleeping."

"Why didn't you tell me?" He leaned in close on the countertop with Miss Venus on the other side making more cotton candy. "I could have helped him."

"You needed to leave him alone," she smiled. "You couldn't have done anything for him. Cleo had to do that. Oracles wake other oracles. I woke her."

He nodded, "I'm very confused on what the roles are in this new scenario. The Wire is focusing him and PJ and seem to not even know about Ray and Calliope."

"I'd say that is a good thing. However, I believe that while this new oracle slept that Ray was undetectable. Every god has their oracle."

"Kendall, the boy's name is Kendall."

"Kendall, I like that." She smiled, "It's a good name."

"What's PJ's role?" asked Fletcher. "She's the one I was led to. Was it only to find Kendall?"

"Who can say? The future is fluid even for an oracle. We only deal with possibilities." She stuck a paper cone in the cotton candy machine and swirled up a pink puffy cloud. "Things may accelerate quickly. Be alert." She put the candy in a bag and hung it up, "Tell me, do you trust Jesse?"

He hesitated. "Yes, I do trust him. Why?"

"Just the fluidity of visions, that's all." Miss Venus took another cone and swirled it up. "So, on another note, do you believe Nemesis will return soon?"

"I feel it," he confessed. "I do. She may already be here somewhere."

"Don't fall in love with her again," she grinned.

"What makes you think I ever stopped?" Fletcher closed his bag of candy. "I think I need something a little stronger."

He stepped away from the van window. Fletcher lifted his aperture that had so many mysterious dials, cogs, and clockwork. He turned one silver button, then another. He watched as Miss Venus vanished into nothingness, and the van aged rapidly until it was a rusted hulk. The sky wiped away like dirt on a window and revealed that he was actually in a simple room that housed the remains of the ice cream truck.

He was down here again. Miss Venus died years ago. Fletcher wasn't even sure why he kept the van. One thing was clear, though; it was dangerous to invoke Miss Venus' memories through the Veil. There was no telling what else could hitch a ride on those memories. He hated having to reprimand Jesse. But he was getting more and more confrontational. Now, there was a new oracle. Jesse Nash could read and interpret divinations, and an oracle was only the conduit.

Every god had an oracle. Kendall was surely supposed to be the oracle for Ray, Fletcher was sure of it. The professor anguished. PJ, Kendall, Ray, and Calliope were kids—innocent kids. They didn't ask for any of it. Maybe Jesse was correct, and they should be told everything. They would be aware instead of ignorant. That information could be so overwhelming, though. Destructive. The last girl he thought was meant to be a living arm of the Veil was told everything, and it destroyed her. Carmen had been carefully spoon-fed limited amounts of information as she discovered it on her own. After all, that has always been the way. This time was different, though. Carmen was destined to be the Veil's human appendage, but all the signs pointed to an additional destiny for her. She was to also be the vessel of Nemesis.

He looked at the rusted, sad, stooped ice cream van. "I wish you really were here right now, Miss Venus."

Fletcher adjusted some dials on his watch and stood back as the shadows in front of him turned liquid. He sighed, and walked headlong into the void, and it closed behind him.

"Where's Poppy? I need to talk to her."

In repose, Poppy sat in a room deep within Oracle Tattoo. The floor was dirt, like an ancient wine cellar, and there was heavy moisture in the air. Fletcher had said at one time it was used to smuggle whiskey from Windsor into Detroit. She could smell the mold, and she would have picked another room, but Poppy didn't want to risk any attention. People can overhear not just with their ears or eyes, oracles can overhear magic. She did not want to be overheard.

The density of the soil, and the extra moisture, enhanced her dampening spell. She needed to practice in solitude, silence, imagined sanity. Poppy put her hands on the soil and whispered four magic words: east, south, west, north.

That was the ancient order of utterance. Sun rises in the east, gives us day in the south, twilight in the west, and Mother Night to the north. Poppy wanted that, the solace of Mother Night. After these hundreds of years of her unusual prison, Mother Night did not judge or beseech, just offer peace.

Four flames erupted from the ground at exact intervals of one quarter, and on an invisible circle three feet in circumference. Three she whispered. The magic number of power. Father. Son Holy Ghost. Maiden. Mother. Crone. Piper. Pru. Phoebe.

"Concentrate," she hissed at herself with disappointment.

Under her breath she repeated: east, south, west, north. Mother Night come forth. Again. East, south, west, north. Mother Night come forth. For two hours, Poppy chanted and adjured. Her persistence paid off, and the gentle swaths of lacy dark green crept from the earth. Her hands were shrouded and comforted. Then, her arms up to her elbows.

"Hey, this isn't right," said Poppy as she saw the green color being consumed by a brownish, undulating lace. "Oh, no you don't."

Poppy squirmed and pulled her arms free. Suddenly, the brown erupted from the soil again only now forming human hands attempting to capture her. She whispered a few words and one of the hands turned to brittle shells from which she broke free. Poppy got to her feet an instant before two more hands shot up looking for her feet.

"I taught you that spell. Fuck you, you won't get me with

it." Poppy watched as the room began to fill with the hands gripping, fingers-rolling. She repeated the whispered words and all the hands turned to brittle egg shells. Then, she popped her tongue and the noise caused all the hands to crumble. She sighed.

Poppy considered getting a joint and going upstairs, but she didn't want to be a part of that boiling mess. Fletcher always meant well, but he could surely create chaos where there should be none. He got that from his father's side, Poppy was sure of it.

She stepped out of the room and exhaled. They were getting too close to locating her place of self-exile. She wanted to be anonymous. Who could show their faces? Worse, Poppy knew the shade that was leveled at her. It was none of their fucking business and they knew it.

Poppy sighed and leaned back against the cool walls so deep inside Oracle Tattoo. She had to give props to Fletcher for coming up with this idea for a Scholar Campus. It was totally undetected—until Fletcher started getting what she thought was sloppy. He was good, but not that good.

Suddenly, a hand shot out and across her mouth. Two others pinned her to the wall. Then, as quickly as they appeared, they pulled Poppy inside until the wall was flat again. As swiftly has that happened, Poppy emerged in a particularly dark, sinister part of a deep forest. She recognized it. Mother Night. The hands vanished, and Poppy stood looking at a stone bench in front of a large comforting fire. A person sat there on the bench, smiling.

"Long time, no see." The woman with burgundy robes and flowers in her hair raised her hands, one holding wine glasses and the other a bottle. "Riesling. Your favorite."

"What do you want, Esme?"

"You know after all these hundreds of years, I have kept your secret shame location private. You know I already think that is so stupid…anyway…come sit and have wine with me. Let's catch up."

"I don't want to catch up," said Poppy. "My departing words

were clear: I will be in exile. My shame is too deep and until I can get the curse lifted from my shoulders, I will remain in solitude."

"I remember, but that was a long time ago. Things have changed."

"No they haven't. I'm unplugged from the grid, but I'm not without ways of finding out what is going on."

"Okay, then you know something is going on."

Poppy exhaled, feeling a little stupid. "Duh, yes something is going on. There are new gods emerging. And then there is the return of…The Hammer…a new enforcer."

"That's troubling," she looked to the fire. "Please, come sit and have some wine and I will tell you what has truly happened. And that we need you."

"Need me, for what?" Poppy walked over. Esme poured. "There is nothing the coven can't do without me that they can do with me."

"Be that as it may, you are one of our most powerful elders…" Esme hesitated, sure Poppy was going to crack the wine bottle over her head. "Not in body. Um, sorry."

"Don't worry about it," said Poppy. "I'm trying to fix it and I think I am close."

"Do you still have the same plan?" asked Esme before she sipped her wine.

"More or less," answered Poppy.

"That is not going to work. I told you that before. Ingratiating yourself to Nemesis when she returns will not make her lift the curse upon you. She may even get more angry and turn you into a tree like she did the boy you were fooling around with."

"We weren't fooling around. We were in love."

"You were in love with the consort of Nemesis, how did you think that was going to play out?"

Poppy sighed. "It does sound stupid. I don't know what I'm thinking. She may never return."

"That's where you are wrong, she is coming back." Esme

finished her glass and filled it again. "I volunteered to come persuade you to rejoin your sisters. We need all the magic we can get. The astrologers have seen signs as well as the tea leaf readers: something big is coming."

"What is it?"

"We think Mother Earth is about to give birth."

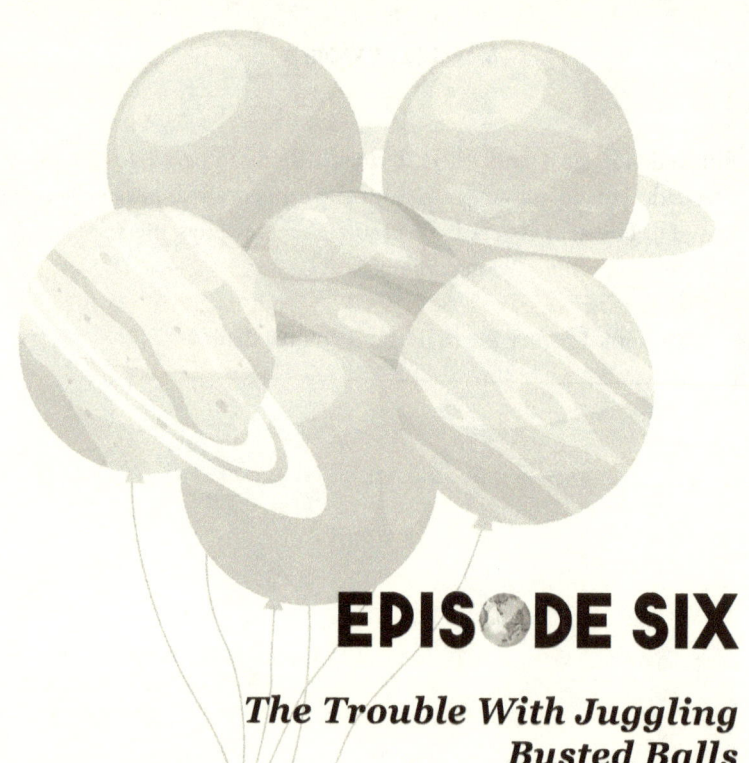

EPIS⊕DE SIX

The Trouble With Juggling Busted Balls

Poppy walked up the stairs from the lower sections of Oracle Tattoo. Only she and few others knew the depths of the vaults and passages. She digested the news Esme gave her. She wasn't sure if she believed it. Who ever heard of a planet giving birth? However, the time to hide was indeed over. There was no choice, no avoiding what was happening above ground. Shit was going down, and Poppy needed a better plan. If Nemesis was returning, perhaps she wouldn't remember imprisoning Poppy in the body of a girl. That would be a bonus. She really didn't know who Poppy was back in her temple really—just another little acolyte attendant serving a goddess.

"Um," Kendall pointed in the direction of the back rooms, "you guys see the little girl standing there too, right? Or is it just me?"

Everyone turned to stare. Poppy smoothed out her skirt and

fidgeted with the bow in her hair.

"Are you lost?" asked PJ. "Can we call your mom?"

Poppy rolled her eyes, "Fuck you. My mom's been dead for 636 years."

Kendall's mouth dropped open, a second later he coughed and laughed all at once. "Oh, gurl."

"What, Peter Pan?"

"Well, that was a classic Poppy entrance," commented Nash. "Done hiding?"

"Fuck you, too," said Poppy. "Where's Fletcher?"

"What's going on?" asked Carmen. "Poppy?"

Poppy went to her friend, "I'm here. I have missed you. You okay?"

"Yeah, I missed you, too."

Poppy looked her over, scrutinizing her face and eyes. "You're the only one I missed."

"Wait, who are you?" asked PJ.

"She's a witch." It was Cleo who answered. "She's a very old cursed witch in a little girl's body."

"Thank you for putting it so succinctly," said Poppy.

"And she's got a hell of a vocabulary," smiled Cleo. "Where have you been?"

"I had to…get away. I needed a break after you came back," she looked over at Carmen. "I'm glad you're okay. I was worried when you came out of the Veil."

"I don't remember any of it," said Carmen. "I just woke up here. I was told you got me here."

Poppy nodded, "You're welcome."

"What is this Veil you all keep talking about?" asked PJ. "You've said it a bunch of times. And I haven't forgotten about the Wire. It's on my list and I never let things go."

Kendall sighed. "That's true. She never…ever…ever let's things go."

Poppy went over to the counter and walked behind it. "I knew I could count on you, Fletcher." She took out the bottle of whiskey and poured some in a paper cup.

"Hey!" Kendall pointed and almost said something, but Poppy's glare shut him up.

"Ah, the Veil," sighed Carmen. "It's like the blood of the universes. There are more than one. A lot more. I don't know how else to describe it. I guess I know it better than anyone here."

Poppy laughed, "Oh, honey, no." She drank the liquor. "You have no clue. None of you little piss whores know anything."

Nash could sense the escalation, "We're all going to stop right now. Shit is starting and we don't need a pissing contest about who has it worse off than anyone else."

"I think we are entitled to answers," said PJ. "We're just kids, you said it yourself. We shouldn't be here."

"I don't want you here," said Poppy, then she drank.

Nash reached for more whiskey. "And I am going to stop you right there. I know you think you know a lot, but you said it. You are just a kid. You have no idea."

"Then why don't you tell us?" PJ snapped. "Or I can just call my mom and tell her this hipster dude kidnapped us."

"He kidnapped me," interrupted Kendall. "And I'm okay with it, really." He smiled at Nash. "Really, I am."

"Teenagers," he sighed, frustrated. "Look, it's not for me to say anything because I'll say it wrong, probably."

"How about her?" PJ pointed at Cleo, "She seems to have it together."

Cleo laughed, "You're funny."

"No, really." PJ was getting more and more frustrated. "You people have dropped what is the equivalent of a nuclear shit bomb on us, and then get mad because we want answers?" She pointed at Kendall, "You tried to tattoo him, and the ink disappeared into his skin. Two guys tried to kill me! Don't forget that."

"She won't let you forget that," Kendall said to Nash who just nodded.

Just then, the door opened, and Fletcher walked in. He paused, slowly taking in the odd collection of characters gathered: two teenagers, a cursed child-witch, an angry hot hipster tattooist, a blind interdimensional fighter, and an oracle.

"Where have you been?" demanded Nash. "You left me alone."

"Nice to see you, too." He looked over at Poppy. "Nice to see you've decided to join us again."

"What can I say, I missed the booze."

PJ approached him, more aggressively than she meant to be. "We need some answers. You are not the guy I thought you were. You're a liar."

"Yeah, I am." He went over to the sofa and sat. "I guess the wave is almost on us." He really wasn't addressing anyone in the room and seemed to be talking more to himself. "I wasn't sure, and then the pieces kept falling together. The future is here."

"What does that mean?" asked PJ.

"It means, I'm going to tell you all that I can. Better to be informed, right?" He laughed. "Today is tomorrow's yesterday."

"Is this an abstinence talk…" Kendall raised his palm. "I already lost my virginity to Jason Smith."

"Jason Smith, really?" asked PJ. "You never told me that. He's a hottie. Congrats. I never would have thought he was gay."

"He says he's bi, but you know gurl…lacrosse players. All over TikTok." Kendall winked.

"We can talk about that later," said PJ. "Before you came in, we were being told what the Veil was—an unseen force like, um, the Force."

"That's a good start," said Fletcher. "Do you understand it?"

She nodded and looked at Kendall, "I kind of understand the metaphor of a bloodstream and stuff…but tell us more."

"There is a big change coming to the Earth, to human beings, to everything," said Fletcher. "We are about to see the return of *gods*."

"Gods?" Kendall was incredulous. "Like the dad of Jesus?"

Fletcher shook his head, "No, like Zeus and Odin."

"Cool!" Kendall held up his palm to PJ, "High five! Chris Hemsworth!"

"No high five," said the professor. "Those guys that are trying to kill you—they don't want new gods coming to the earth. They like things the way they are."

"What are these gods, I don't understand? Are they people?"

"They are people, but they're gods," added Nash.

"So, is it Odin, or Thor?" asked Kendall. "Please let it be Thor."

"No, those gods are gone. Only in rare circumstances can they ever return or would want to return. Those gods are called persistent gods and they usually have a deep connection to the Earth or humans."

"Through the Veil? That's where they coming from?" asked PJ.

"Yes, through the bloodstream of the universe." Fletcher paused to gather his thoughts, "Look this is a huge topic and I don't expect you to get it all at once. But you all are here to play a role, as am I." He turned to Kendall, "You are an oracle to one of the new gods. Every god has an oracle."

"Which one? Who?"

"I don't know," replied Fletcher. "We're in a strange period where they will start to emerge. We need to help them. We need to help them hide from the assassins who want to kill them before they really understand who they are."

"The Wire? They want to kill them? Why now? Why gods? Are you sure?" asked PJ.

"My skeptical student," he smiled. "I am glad you question so much. Yes, that is what the Wire wants to do. Kill them before they become the gods they were born to be. Right now, though, do not question too much. You're going to see and experience some remarkable and strange things from here on out. All of you are. I know it may be very frustrating, but I don't have all the answers. No one does."

"How many times has this happened?" asked Kendall.

"I mean that new gods came along."

"There is no pattern that any of the scholars can detect, only that they are an extension of the universe. Just like any other extension of the universe. Human beings are a manifestation of the universe."

"Squirrels?" commented Kendall.

"Even squirrels," laughed Nash.

"So here is what I want you to do," began Fletcher, "just go home and live. There is no way to know when things will happen. It could be weeks, or years. You are protected by the rune."

"So, the Wire. I think I get it now," said PJ. "But why do they want to kill the gods?"

"The last god was killed by the Wire a little over 2,000 years ago. The Wire has controlled people ever since with false faith. If a real god came along, they'd lose that power. So here we are…"

"Time has no dominion over the Veil," added Carmen. "It is going to do what it is going to do."

"So, the Wire will not be able to find us?" asked PJ.

"Correct. They can't find you and Kendall, but if you go around and being obvious they could detect someone else. So, don't do it. Stay under the radar." answered Nash. "The runes I tattooed on you will hide you. I bet you won't even show up on a security camera."

"Cool," grinned Kendall. "How about in a locker room?" Everyone grew silent and just stared at him. "What? It's a legitimate question."

Kendall sat in the cafeteria at school. PJ was with him. She was glued to her phone, reading and tapping. He sighed. "Hey, I need some attention here."

"What?" her reply was vacuous.

"I am wearing new sneaks and you haven't said a word," he griped. "Prada?"

She paused and looked down at them. "Oh, nice." Then she returned to her phone.

"OMG, what are you reading anyway?"

"I can't believe you are so calm after what happened yesterday."

"What's there to get excited about?" he said. "I mean, you heard what the professor said: it could be years before anything happened. And we're all protected and literally invisible. Life as normal, I'd say." He got up and got closer to PJ, "Personally, I want to test the limits of this not being detectible."

She stopped and just looked at him. "It doesn't mean you're invisible, dork." She rolled her eyes. "What are you going to do, rob a bank? Steal some new shoes?"

He wasn't looking at PJ; he was looking across the lunch-room. "Maybe see if that hot boy can see me if I watched him in the shower."

"Don't be a Weinstein. Hashtag *Me Too*? Anyway, who do you want to see?" PJ followed his eyes over to Ray Kellan sitting with the new girl. "Really? Ray Kellan? You think he would not pull your own arm off and beat you to death with it?"

"Oh, come on. He totally sets off my radar," said Kendall. "What are you reading?"

"I'm doing research on all this secret stuff, but I can't really find anything."

"I doubt that all that secret shit that happened is going to be on Google." He paused, "Do you hear that?"

"Hear what? You being a perv?"

"That buzzing," he said. "I heard it earlier today, but it went away. It's getting louder again, though. And my stomach feels gross like I'm going to hurl."

"Maybe you're pregnant."

"Fuck you, I'm being serious." He snapped.

It wasn't like Kendall to be so coarse. PJ put her phone down. "Do you have a fever?" She checked him. "You're not warm."

"No, I feel dizzy, too. Not dizzy, like I can hear a TV and that high-pitched tone if it is not on a channel."

"That's weird." PJ took a few dollars out of her pocket, "Here, go over there and get a Vernor's. It will settle your stomach."

"Vernor's is medicine, good idea," said Kendall as he took the money.

The vending machine with soda was to the left of where Ray and Calliope were quietly talking and giggling. Their friendliness irritated Kendall. Ray Kellan could not seriously be into the new girl. She was so fake: she should just throw her naked body on him. The pitchy buzz amplified as he got closer. Kendall kept going, though. He shook his head to clear it. Ray casually glanced up as Kendall went to the vending machine; they shared a smile, their eyes snagged on each other's for a quick second before it broke. Then, Ray returned his attention to Calliope.

"If that's my gaydar going off…" he said while feeding a dollar into the machine. It spit back out, "Fuck. Go in." He lined up the dollar again, and the rollers pulled it in. Then Kendall fed the second bill into the machine.

Suddenly, the buzz magnified seemingly exponentially. The tone's pitch tortured Kendall. He grabbed his ears, his head, as an unseen drill penetrated his skull. Down he went, to his knees then to prone.

"Dude!" Ray saw Kendall go down and jumped to help him. "Are you okay?" Kendall was unresponsive; his eyes rolled back and only the whites were showing. "I think he's having a seizure! Someone call 911!"

Ray was trying to clear the area, but Kendall clutched him like a vice. Images flooded Kendall's brain as their skin touched; vivid flashes; wailing and quaking. Melting watercolor images washed over his body, obscuring what vision he still possessed. Sweat soaked through his clothes. Finally, he fought back to consciousness. Kendall was able to open his eyes and they locked on Ray's for the second time in a few moments.

"It's you," Kendall whispered. "Mother fucker."

"It's me, Ray." He replied, not grasping the gravity of the

statement. "Can you understand me? You having a seizure? I think someone called 911."

The moment had passed, and Kendall went flaccid. He was conscious, but lethargic. PJ ran over when she saw the seizure unfold. Her first instinct was Kendall's safety, and as she knelt by her friend, she knew what it was.

"It's him," Kendall said. "It's him." PJ looked at Ray.

"Hey, I didn't do anything," Ray put his hands up like he was under arrest and stood. "He just wigged out."

"It's okay," said PJ. "Don't worry about it. I got this. He's a little disoriented."

A circle of students gathered around, and the security guard came over as well. Kendall was sitting up on his own by the time someone from the administration arrived. He didn't want any help and asked them to leave him alone. That didn't get far, and the administrators and security officer escorted him away from the scene.

"What was that?" Ray asked PJ as she hung back for a minute.

"Not sure," she was trying to think of something quickly. *Ray? Ray Kellan? WTF?* "He's dehydrated. He's trying to cut weight for swimming, and he's been starving himself."

"Swimmers don't cut weight," Ray said with skepticism. "Is he on drugs?"

"No, he isn't on drugs," snapped PJ. "I gotta go check on him."

PJ rushed out of the lunchroom in the direction of the administrative offices. An ambulance had pulled up outside, but thankfully there were no sirens—just lights. Ray stood with his hands on his hips and exhaled. Calliope had joined him.

"What was that all about?" she asked.

"Kid had a seizure, I think."

"Do you know him? He seemed to be totally into you."

"Nah, I don't think so. I know his friend, though. She was on my little league team."

"Come on," said Calliope. "The bell's about to ring. I'm

sure he will be fine."

As they went off to class, PJ walked down the hall to the administrative offices. There, in the small nurse's room, Kendall sat upright and was drinking water. The nurse was speaking to his mom on the phone and allowed PJ to enter.

"Are you okay?" she asked.

"What a rush," he replied. "It was like electricity."

"What happened?"

He sighed, gathering his thoughts. "It's so hard to describe. I had this buzzing in my ears, and it was like a mix of voices, bees, horns, everything. Then when I got closer to Ray, it got to be too much, and I lost it. The next thing I knew, he was helping me. Our skin touched, and that's when I knew it was Ray."

"Is that bad or good?"

"I don't know—just sounds and visions."

The nurse came over to them. "Your mother is on her way. Kendall, are you feeling better?" He nodded. "The EMT is still going to look at you and see if you have to go in." She handed him a sealed cup, "Unfortunately, I have to get a urine sample."

"He's not on drugs," said PJ.

"It's school policy, dear," said the nurse. "I'm sure he's not. But I have to do it."

"It's okay, I don't mind." Kendall took the cup from her.

Just then, the EMTs came in the room. There were two of them: one young, blond guy who barely looked like he was out of high school; and an older black woman who was all business.

"Hi," she said with a smile, "Are you Kendall?"

"Yeah, I'm the fainter."

"I'm Karen," she said. "This is Parker. We're going to take a look at you."

Parker was talking with the nurse while Karen attended to Kendall. "Have you ever had a seizure before?" She pulled out a flashlight. "I'm going to check your eyes now." She tested his pupils for a healthy reaction. "Any history of fainting? Did you fall and hit your head recently?"

"No," replied Kendall. "You're name is really Karen?"

He was ignored. "Do you take any drugs, prescriptions or other?"

"No." He held up the specimen cup. "I'm sure this will prove it."

Karen smiled. "You're athletic. Are you a runner or swimmer?"

"Swimmer."

"Any changes to your practices? Physical activity? Taking any supplements like caffeine?"

"Just coffee."

Karen nodded, "That's good, just caffeine."

"Thanks, Karen."

Parker came over to join them. "Hello, I'm Parker." He scrutinized Kendall head to toe. There was a curious look on his face.

"What?" Kendall immediately noticed and became insecure.

"Your blood pressure is normal according to the nurse, so I'm wondering about the ringing in your ears. Are they ringing now?"

Kendall shook his head, "Not really."

Parker studied Kendall, "I think you should come with us."

PJ's suspicious nature aroused. "To the hospital?"

Parker glanced at Karen. "To the emergency room."

"His mom will be here like any minute."

PJ went to the window and looked out at the ambulance parked at the front of the building. There was no designation of the township, city, or any private ambulance company that she could recognize. Parker was trying to lead Kendall to a standing position. Karen joined him.

From outside in the hall, the football coach entered unexpectedly. "I heard you were in here, Kendall."

"From who?"

"Ray told me." The coach looked at the EMTs. "How is he?"

Parker let go of Kendall's arm. "We think he should go to the emergency room. Get some tests."

"I called his parents and they're on the way," said the coach. "They can take him."

Karen glanced at Parker again. "We can take him. The school called us, and it is our responsibility."

"His parents will be here in five minutes. I'll make sure they take him over." The coach went to Kendall, taking a protective stance between him and the EMTs. "I've already talked to Principal Owens. He is going to meet Kendall's parents and escort them here. It's okay, you can go. I'm sure there is someone who really needs you out there somewhere."

"Like a baby being born, or something, Karen. Seriously, you should slap your mom for that," added Kendall.

The EMTs left the building and sat in the ambulance. PJ was watching them from the window. The nurse had also left the room, leaving the three of them alone in the office.

"Coach," she began, "I don't know what is going on, but thank you. There is something wrong with those two paramedics."

"Kendall, PJ, don't freak out, but I didn't call your parents." He took out his phone and showed Kendall the screen. "I know Dr. Fletcher. I need both of you to get out of here ASAP."

"What do you mean?" PJ was shocked. "You're the football coach!"

"No time to explain, but I've been a friend of Fletcher's for a long time," he said.

"Where's Ray?" asked Kendall. There was urgency in his voice, "I have to talk to him."

Coach looked out the window, the ambulance had pulled away. "Fuck it." He grabbed them both by the arms, "Come on."

They hurried through the hallways. Kids mulled about, and a few asked questions. Kendall was clear-headed again and ignored everyone wishing him well. They passed down two halls, until they finally entered the weight room where Ray was waiting.

"Coach, what's going on?" asked Ray. "Why did you tell me to wait in here?" He saw Kendall, "You okay, man?"

Kendall nodded, "Yeah, I'm good." He winced. The buzz was returning. His knees buckled, but PJ and the coach held him up.

"You're not okay," Ray moved to help him. He reached down and caught Kendall before he could fall to the ground.

The connection was solid. *Made*. Kendall cried out. The back of his light-colored shirt was wet and inky black. Ray pulled off Kendall's shirt. His smooth skin was no longer pale but stained with an image. It moved. It shifted.

"What the fuck is going on!" screamed Ray.

PJ ignored him. She looked at the image. "There. In the picture. It's us. And others. They have guns." With eyes wide, "We have to get out of here. They're coming to kill us!"

Kendall nodded. "She's right. The noise is going away. When you told me what it was—it made the sound stop."

Ray held up Kendall's shirt; it was white again. "I don't know what's going on, but here. We're going to get Calliope and get out of this school."

"They're not after her," stated PJ. "They're after you."

"Me?" Ray was dumbfounded. "Why?"

"Because of what you can do, and who you are?"

Ray dropped Kendall and backed away. The defensive glow surged around his body. "What are you talking about?"

"I'm your oracle," said Kendall as he put on his shirt. "You're a god, okay?"

"I wasn't going to tell him like that," said PJ.

"Oh, come on." Kendall sobered. "Look at him. Of course, he's a god. And he has some kind of power probably."

"Wait, wait," Rays hands glowed. "This is all wrong."

"See, he has power," said Kendall. "Totally not surprised. Abs and power."

"We're going to all die if we don't get out of here," PJ opened the door to the weight room. "Where is Calliope?"

"She has biology this hour."

"Okay, biology. Let's go." PJ scanned the hall. "It's quiet. I think we're cool."

Suddenly, the fire alarms sounded. Shrill screams and panicked, hustling footsteps followed. Outside, students were out of control. They were running. Then, there was the dull popping sound of guns.

"There's a shooter!" PJ slammed the door. "We have to hide."

"No." Ray grabbed the door and opened it. "We can't let anyone get hurt. We have to find Calliope."

Kendall and PJ tried to protest, but Ray was already in the hall. He was using his body to push through the students, moving towards the biology and science labs. The gunfire was at the other end of the school. Kendall pushed through behind Ray, and PJ was following. Students were ducking into classrooms and barring the doors as best they could. He kept going, though, shoving students aside.

Finally, they made it to the biology lab. Inside, the students were huddled beneath the heavy metal desks. Ray looked back down the hall; two figures in black were coming. They shot two students who were unlucky enough to be in the hall.

"Get in the room!" Ray opened the glass door and shoved Kendall inside. He snatched PJ by the arm, "You too."

"Ray?" Calliope stood up from behind one of the counters. "Oh my God, Ray! Get in here! There's someone shooting up the school!"

"I know," he looked back down the hall. "I can see them. They're coming. No matter what, keep this door shut."

He turned, planted his feet, and readied himself. Kendall said he was a god. How did he survive a plane crash? How did he survive being hit by a car? He knew. Kendall knew. PJ knew. The figures at the end of the hall paused. They probably knew, too. One popped out a magazine and replaced it. They had on dark ski masks, they were dressed in black clothes, and each appeared to have on a Kevlar vest.

"You're done!" shouted Ray. "You aren't going to kill anyone else."

"We'll see who is standing at the end. All of you will fall!"

shouted one of them and aimed his weapon. "For the Wire!"

The trigger released. Streams of bullets exploded out of the military-grade muzzle. Many missed the target and impacted the walls. Glass shattered. However, enough of the bullets slammed into Ray to make him stumble. The second assailant began to fire. Each impact, though, simply ricocheted as it hit Ray's body. The golden glow pushed outward from his skin. A shell of impenetrable light expanded like a dawning sun. He raised his open palms, manipulating the shield. No bullet would ever be able to hit him.

The assailants walked towards him, firing. Each round was nothing to Ray. Fluff. Nerf darts. Spit wads. Butterflies. Ray's shield filled the hall, sealing the biology lab safely behind him. Inside the room, kids were pushing against the glass to see what was happening. All they could see was their football star saving them from the shooters.

The bullets stopped. The ammunition failed. The attackers could see there was no way to continue. However, Ray's shield had formed behind them. It was a second layer. They were trapped between the two. Ray concentrated. His two shields contracted closer together, forcing them to walk. One pulled out a pistol and took some shots, but they also were useless. He threw the gun itself at Ray. It deflected.

"Stand down," ordered Ray. "You're not going anywhere. I can do this forever."

The two shooters traded glances. One of them pulled out a hand-grenade. The pin was flipped and fell to the stone floor. Ray lifted one of his palms, and merely thought about the bomb. Another shield formed around the attacker's hand as the grenade exploded. The hand was destroyed, but the bomb did no other damage. Raging with pain, the masked assailant fell to the hall floor and onto a pile of empty bullet casings. The other one looked down the hall at Ray.

"You will not live for long," said a woman's voice from beneath the ski mask.

"I'm holding you for the police."

She held up her hands. "You'll be discovered. The world will know your secret."

"I don't care anymore," said Ray. "I can't let you get away with this."

"Ray," it was Calliope. "I want to take off her mask."

"No, are you nuts? If I lower the shield she will shoot you. She can't shoot me."

"I can take care of myself, and you know it." Calliope tried to touch him, but he was surrounded by the force field. "I can't touch you if you keep the shield up. Lower it, I want to make sure you're okay."

"No, I can't."

"Put one around them, like you did the grenade." Calliope pointed to the figure on the floor, "I think he's dead. Look at all the blood. His hand got blown off."

"I can't."

"Fine, then put one around her. Let me go help him. He's bleeding to death if he isn't dead already."

Ray looked at Calliope. Her voice was measured and reasonable. She looked at him with vulnerable eyes that twinkled with her electrical plasma. Tiny balls of light were running down her face, down her exposed arms, dripping off her fingers. She could take care of herself.

He raised his other hand, and a new bubble formed around the standing figure. Then, he lowered his other hand and the other shields vanished. Calliope cautiously walked towards the fallen person, carefully keeping her eye on the trapped one.

"You, too?" the stranger said. "Magic? Lightning? What is that?"

"Shut up, or you'll find out."

"You both will be exposed." The sound of sirens wailed outside. "Everyone will know. They will lock you up."

"I said shut up." Calliope raised her open hand; balls of glowing plasma massed in her hand.

Suddenly, the coach came from behind Ray. "I was in the other lab."

"It's okay, the police are coming. I don't have to hide anymore."

"Yeah, you do. Sorry about this." The coach then hit Ray as hard as he could with a large pink golf umbrella he had in his hand.

The force field around the other attacker collapsed and she immediately reached for a gun.

"Fuck you." Calliope growled.

An iridescent stream of light made of thousands of static electrical plasma balls covered the woman. They exploded, releasing their charges simultaneously. The smell of frying flesh and burning hair permeated the hall. Calliope looked down at the wounded attacker; he was still alive. With a mere thought, another stream of plasma burned him to a crisp.

"Wow," said the coach from behind. "I didn't expect that. Come on, we have to go."

Ray was rubbing his head, staggering to a standing position. "Why did you do that?"

"We have to go!" Coach pulled at Ray.

"What about PJ and Kendall?" asked Ray.

"Leave them," he said.

"No way," said Ray. "I'm not leaving them behind." He rushed into the lab to locate them. "No telling what will happen if I leave them behind, so they are coming with us."

"How are we going to get out, the cops have it locked down," said Calliope.

The coach opened the umbrella, "The professor thought of that. We need to stay under this, and no one can see us."

With PJ and Kendall located, they left the building unseen.

Ray held a bag of frozen broccoli to his head, "You didn't have to hit me, coach."

"Sorry, I had to stop you from doing..." he raised his hands and gestured, "...whatever you were doing. We had to get out of there."

They were in *Oracle Tattoo*. Calliope sat on the sofa and they watched the TV coverage of the shooting. Next to her, was Ray. The coach paced nervously. Fletcher and Nash were also watching the TV along with Poppy, who was less interested than the others. Cleo and Carmen were there watching.

"What about Kendall and PJ?" asked Ray. Then he looked directly at them. "You guys won't say anything, right?"

"They won't say a word," commented Fletcher. "He's your oracle. And PJ is loyal."

"Yeah, I won't say anything," said Kendall. "Neither will she, right?"

"I don't even know what I saw," said PJ. "And I'd appreciate it if you'd stop talking like we aren't here. We are here and we are up to our asses in this."

Ray lowered the thawing bag of produce. "My oracle. He said that, too. What is that? Why are we here?"

"You're here because you're a god," said Calliope. "Weren't you paying attention? So am I apparently."

"Don't get ahead of yourself," commented Poppy.

"Excuse me?" Calliope looked at Fletcher and Nash, "Who does this little rude girl belong to?"

"I don't belong to anyone, honey." It was Poppy who answered her question.

"Shut up, you guys!" Carmen had the remote and turned up the sound. "I'm trying to hear."

"What's to hear? The Wire found out where Ray was and tried to kill him. Pity, they probably didn't know what he could do."

Carmen turned the sound even louder. The anchor cut away to the reporter who was giving an eyewitness report. Two attackers entered the school and began shooting students and staff with what is suspected to be military weapons before blowing themselves up. It is not certain if they meant to commit suicide or if it was an accident, but the attackers are dead. Authorities have locked down the campus. So far, there are multiple fatalities and injuries. That is all we know at this time.

"It will be a long time before we really know anything," said Cleo. She turned and looked at Ray, "So, you're him."

Ray was more frozen than the vegetables in the bag.

"Yes, this is him," interjected Fletcher.

"You guys are freaking him out," added Nash. "You're freaked out, right?"

"Yeah, kinda." He turned to the coach. "What the fuck? Who are you?"

"I've been watching and protecting you for a long time, son."

"They like to kill them when they're young," said Poppy bluntly. "You know, before they realize who they are and that they can probably kill a stupid human with a thought."

Calliope wrinkled her nose distastefully and glared at Poppy. "Who are you?"

"Let's do a round of introductions, maybe that will help." The little girl grinned. "I'm a cursed witch trapped in a little girl's body. That girl there," she pointed at Cleo, "is the oracle for the goddess Nemesis, who cursed me because I dared love a boy she wanted. And that one next to her," she pointed at Carmen, "is a blind girl who can go into the Veil and fight like a badass." She pointed at Nash, "He's an asshole and the apprentice to the bigger asshole. Nash and Fletcher."

"Thank you, Poppy," said Fletcher. "We get it. That's enough." He sighed. "I'm sorry it happened this way."

"You're always sorry," said Carmen.

Fletcher let the slight go unanswered. "It was bound to happen, that you'd be discovered, but no one knew how. Your coming has been prophesized for hundreds of years. Thousands."

"I'm not anything." Ray put the broccoli back on his head. "For shits and giggles, let's just say it's true. If I'm the next one, what happened to the last ones?"

"It's a pretty common story," said Nash. "Ever heard of Jesus?"

"What?" PJ looked over.

Kendall was also surprised. "Yeah, um...What?"

"It's true," began Fletcher. "The Old Testament was the prediction. The New Testament was the arrival. Of course, those stories are cherry-picked to create a convenient myth to keep people under control. The whole story is much, much deeper. You see, Jesus Christ was the first of what was to be a new coming of gods to the earth. However, the Wire, in whatever iteration they were at the time, was able to discover him and kill him."

"Why would they kill him?" asked PJ.

"A real god can bring people together. The people will listen and follow them, instead of following the dominant male leaders of any given human culture. So, once they killed him, they constructed a myth and created the three major religions to control the people who still believed the spirit of the god was viable."

"So, you're saying God is dead?"

"Alive and dead. Many times. Sometimes the same one, but not usually. It's complicated."

"They killed Jesus," echoed Ray. "The same people you say are trying to kill me."

"That's totally messed up," commented Kendall.

"Yeah, it is." Ray put the broccoli down. "I don't know what all this is yet, but that just sounds ridiculous."

"You're a different kind of god for this world," said Fletcher. "You're indestructible. They cannot kill you. They've tried."

"Bullshit," Ray looked away from him, embarrassed. "This isn't a power anyone would want. I hurt people. You don't know anything."

"I know you survived the plane crash—because you're indestructible. We have been watching and protecting you all your life." He pointed at Calliope, "Then you came along. So, there are two of you to protect."

"I can protect myself," snapped Calliope as plasma balls danced on her fingernails.

"But your temper and jealousy make you volatile—and vulnerable," said Fletcher. "Yes, I know your parents very well, too."

"You're the one who arranged for my dad's jobs when I…" she looked ashamed, "…when I lost control."

Fletcher nodded. "Yes, we had to make sure you stayed safe, too. It isn't often we have two rise simultaneously. You are *skyborne*, Calliope. And you are *earthborne*, Ray."

"What does that mean?" asked Ray.

"It means that there are certain creatures on this planet that are either *skyborne*, *earthborne*, or *starborne*. All are special. All have a specific alignment to the universe. They are connected to each other, too. Like two *earthbornes* will be able to vibe with each other."

"Like twins have a special language?" asked Kendall.

"Yeah, it can be like that," replied Fletcher. "I don't know many who are a *nativeborne* person—or creature—so my knowledge on that is limited."

"So I'm a rare bird?" asked Calliope.

"I think you're *starborne*," Poppy said to Calliope, "but that's just my opinion."

Fletcher ignored the statement. "We have plenty of time to figure that out, but the reality is: the gods are here now. There will be more. And so will the assassins who want to kill you."

"Why do they want to kill them again? I'm not sure if I'm following. Hey, was Karen that masked woman who tried to kill us?" asked Kendall.

"Weren't you paying attention? A real god threatens those in power," said PJ.

"Oh, yeah." Kendall was still worried, "Will they want to kill me, too?"

"Not as much as a god, but they will want to kill you, too because you are the speaker to the gods."

"What does that mean?" asked Calliope. "He's a speaker to the gods?"

"No," it was Cleo that answered. "He's is a speaker to Ray. Each god has an oracle. I am an oracle to the goddess Nemesis, who unfortunately is no longer on this earth."

"What happened to her?" asked Kendall.

"She left," replied Cleo. "She is one of the rare gods that does come and go and transcends time. She is a persistent goddess."

"This is a lot to take in," said Ray.

"It's okay, we'll help you get through it," said Nash. "Want some whiskey? It helps."

"We will get through this," said Fletcher. "Nash here will be your guide. He will tutor you and teach you the history housed in this vault."

"Vault?" Kendall looked around. "It's a tattoo shop."

"It's that, too," said Nash. "But it's really a library. A museum. A sanctuary. A military outpost. We are one of six in the world."

"Where are the others?" asked Kendall.

"Egypt, Bhutan, Thailand, Denmark, Siberia, and Antarctica."

"Antarctica?" PJ glanced at Kendall, "Isn't it a little cold there?"

"The inhospitality makes it perfect," smiled Fletcher. "So, in an awkward segue, I hate to be the bearer of more bad news. You will not be returning to the real world any time soon."

"What about me?" asked coach.

Fletcher forgot he was there. "I think it is too late for you to go back either. You could never explain being missing for 12 hours from the crime scene and then just show up again. You know, they have locked that school down, and went over it with a fine-toothed comb."

"He's right," said Cleo who was on her phone, reading. "It says one teacher and four kids are missing." She smiled, "That would be you four."

"Ya think?" said Kendall.

"We're missing?" asked PJ. "What's that mean?"

"It means we're not going back," surmised Ray. "Is that what you're saying?"

"Yes. The lives you knew are over. You can't go back. There would be too many questions. Your families would be in danger."

"Never?"

"Never."

"But I don't want this," said PJ. "I want to go to school. I want to be a teenager. I want to go to college. I want a normal life. This isn't for me."

"People in hell want ice water," said Carmen. "We don't always get what we want. You think I want to be here? You think I wanted to go blind and fall into the Veil?"

"I'm sorry, I didn't mean anything." PJ took out her phone. "Can I at least say goodbye to my parents?"

"Your phones won't work, sorry."

Kendall pointed at Cleo, "Hers works."

"I can be trusted not to expose us."

"One day, we will try to get a message to your families," said Fletcher. "But not now. Now it is very, very dangerous. Think of them instead of yourselves. Are you okay with them being targets of assassination 24/7?"

"Strangle the baby in its crib, and it can't grow up," said Calliope sarcastically.

"Unfortunately, that is true," agreed Fletcher. "Calliope, I would like to be your mentor."

"Sure," she said. "Are you gonna teach me how to use my powers like Jean Grey?"

"Something like that."

"Well, I don't know about the rest of you but I'm starving," said Kendall. "Can we get some pizzas?"

"Pizzas," said Ray. "That would be awesome. I can kill two myself."

Nash smiled, "I'll get some pizzas."

EPIS DE SEVEN

Learning How to be a God

Time was already blurring, becoming formless. Calliope had no idea how long they truly were in the tattoo shop. Was it a day? A week? What did it really matter? Their phones were useless. She didn't know how Fletcher was able to suspend them, but he did.

She sat on a patio deep within the tattoo shop. It was larger than she ever expected, more like a complex of buildings connected by halls, tunnels, doors, and stairs. It must have taken up the entire block of dilapidated buildings in the rundown neighborhood. A successful secret, without saying. The patio was like an oasis within the complex. There were potted trees, a few benches, and a small fountain with a buddha statue sitting in it. Above, the sky was clear but only the brightest stars could be seen amongst the pollution of city lights.

"Hey," it was Ray coming up from behind. "This is pretty cool."

"I found it a couple days ago. Nice, right?" Calliope gestured to the open sky, "It's so quiet you can't even hear the road."

"That's nice," he said. Ray moved closer and sat on a bench near the fountain. "What a nightmare."

"That's an understatement," agreed Calliope. She made a few plasma balls on her fingernails, "I wonder how long we're going to be kept here. I think we could escape, you know. I could fry everyone with electricity, and you could make a hole in the wall."

"I don't think we're here as prisoners," said Ray. "I think we're here for our own safety."

"We don't need protecting."

Ray considered her words. "Maybe, but I think until we have more information—and can actually understand what we can do—it may be good to lay low."

"Whatever," she let the plasma explode like firecrackers. "It's easy for you to say, they are pegging you as the new Jesus."

"No, I'm not anything like that."

"You heard the stories. He was the first, just like you; but they got to him first and killed him."

"I think that may be the only similarity—not the killing me part but being the first. Hopefully, I'll learn more from my lessons."

"Oh yeah, lessons." She stood and went to the fountain. "You get to work with the hot hipster, and I get the weird professor. I guess he thinks I'm a problem child."

"You are," laughed Ray.

"I know," she laughed too. "You know what I mean. I don't even have an oracle. You do. Maybe I'm not like you—just some kind of freak who makes lightning balls. So, what do you think they'll be teaching us?"

"I don't know. We are going to have dinner tonight, the three of us. Me, Nash, and Kendall."

"Kendall is crushing on you big time."

Ray blushed. "He's cute, but…"

"…but not your type?" Calliope moved closer to him.

"Right, not my type." Ray got nervous as she got closer. "I don't think I'm even thinking of anything like that. I'm so stressed about what's going on."

"Well, I can help you with that stress," she said. "I think I've been pretty obvious how I feel about you, haven't I?"

"What if you blow my dick off?" He laughed, but Calliope did not. "Sorry, I guess that wasn't funny. I'm sorry I'm not responding the way you want. I guess the truth is I'm a coward. At least when it comes to girls."

"I promise you will remember it for the rest of your life." She smiled and touched his muscular arms, "We click. Come on, you know we do."

He demurred. "We do, but I am so weirded out by shit…" Ray pulled away from her. "I'm uncomfortable here."

"No one is around," she said. "No one would see us."

"Someone would see. That strange witch girl is always sneaking around. Really quiet. You never know where she is."

Calliope realized she was getting nowhere with him. "All I know is this is going to get old really fast if something doesn't change. You are totally avoiding me. I'm attractive, I'm not stupid. We would totally be the hot couple in school."

"There is no school anymore, remember?" He moved away from her, and he could tell she was offended. "Listen, I gotta go meet Nash and Kendall for dinner." Ray started for the door leading inside. "I'll talk to you later, though."

"Whatever. Just go. Tell me how it goes," she said as he left the grotto. Then she was alone again. "God, what is fucking wrong with me? With him?"

She turned to listen to the babbling fountain. It was truly quiet and peaceful. Maybe it wasn't so bad being here. No one was going to worry about her, she surmised. Her parents were probably relieved she was out of their hair. No doubt, Fletcher contacted them. But she couldn't be totally confident in that. She had been nothing but trouble for them for as long as she could remember. At least she could make lightning balls. Calliope laughed to herself. Fuck Ray. She didn't need him. Why was she throwing herself at the hottest guy in school again? Because that was her MO. It wasn't really about the guy but being the jealous couple. Any guy would do as long as all the other bitches were jealous and knew who was the alpha. Above her, she heard a crow crying.

Calliope looked up to see it sitting on the rim of the grotto. "Hey, there. Wow, you're huge. Did you hear me thinking that men suck?"

The crow cawed and swooped away. Calliope tried to track the bird but lost it against the sky. She questioned if crows were even active or not at night. It was unusual. With the bird's departure, and Ray's, it was silent again. The fountain was the only sound to hear.

Then, the crow returned. The bird shocked her with its enormous flapping black wings. And it settled in front of her, on the ground in front of the fountain.

"Wow, look at you." Calliope knelt closer to the bird's level. "What are you doing out at night? Do you come out at night?" Its head flicked, the eye blinked like a flash. "Can you understand me?" She laughed.

Suddenly, two more large black birds descended. They circled and flapped and crowed. The new arrivals made Calliope nervous. Horror movies had crows in them. And nothing good happened when they were around.

"Too Edgar Allan Poe for me, shoo," she said and waved her arms. "Go away. You're not killing me or pecking my eyes out." She made a handful of plasma balls, "You wanna be turned into KFC?"

Her demonstration of power seemed to quell the birds. The two landed next to the one that was already on the ground. The three of them looked at her, heads moving like strobe flashes, eyes blinking. Without warning, the two outside birds attacked the middle one. Sniping. Clicking beaks. Snatching at each other. They savagely pecked at its abdomen. Bloody feathers flew. They ripped their brother's exposed skin, trailing the intestines out onto the stone. Curled. Steaming. Sublime. The two remaining birds looked up at Calliope, clicking their beaks. Instead of revulsion, Calliope knelt. There was a message in the entrails. It was swirling, a visage of contrasts.

"My oracles," she whispered. "I can see."

Calliope studied the guts. The image was there: Ray and Nash and Kendall. Three males, three in power. There was no room for her in their rank. Nash and Ray had their hands about each other's waists. Kendall joined the embrace. Then the three kissed savagely, sensually, unashamed.

She didn't understand what it meant. "What are you showing me?"

Once she had glanced away from the entrails the live birds opened their wings and hid their disemboweled brother from her sight. It took only a moment, but when they closed their wings again, he was alive and whole. The three of them flashed their eyes at her and tilted their heads strobe-like, then took to the sky. She would get no answer from them.

Ray returned to his room deep inside the complex of *Oracle Tattoo* after dinner. Like the others, he couldn't quite wrap his head around the depth of the building, the halls, the stairs and passages, and its purpose. Sure, they told him it was some type of outpost for whatever crap they were into. There was more; there were a lot of lies. It was in the walls, and in the air. The whole place stank of secrets.

There was a knock on the door of his small space. Ray sat up in his bed. Nash was in the doorframe.

"You busy?" asked Nash.

"What would I be doing? I'm literally in a dungeon," said Ray. "Come on in."

"I was going to ask how you liked your room." He entered, "At least you got your own bathroom."

"I like that part," replied Ray. "It's not home, though."

"Well, it is now for a while." Ray tracked him like a spotlight, making Nash uncharacteristically nervous. "Dr. Fletcher and I were talking. We know we probably can't get any of your belongings from your house. Your mom has already been safely disappeared and relocated."

"Disappeared?"

Nash nodded and sat on the folding chair next to the IKEA desk they provided for Ray. "The Scholars got there before the police, and fortunately the Wire. She's safe."

"Will I ever see her again?"

"Yeah, of course. Not right away, but you will see her again. No one is going to keep your mother away from you."

"She's not my real mom," said Ray. "My mom died in the plane crash that I survived."

"I know your story well," he said.

"You do, do you?"

"We both do, Dr. Fletcher and I. He's been watching and protecting you since you were recovered. He found you a foster mom through the Scholars."

"These 'Scholars,' who are they? Are you a Scholar?"

Nash paused to arrange his thoughts into words. "I am, but not fully yet. I am Dr. Fletcher's apprentice. One day, I hope to be a professor as well."

"How many professors are there?"

"Quite a few. They're all over the world. Some are super old, some are new. And they all have an acolyte—an assistant."

"Seems like that is a thing around here. Is Kendall my acolyte as you call it?"

Nash shook his head. "No, he is your oracle. He's literally an extension of your senses, but more. He can see the future and interpret it. He is supposed to be your counsel."

"My counsel?" laughed Ray. "We're both nearly kids."

"That's a cop out. You're not too young. That's just a way to avoid responsibility. You'll learn together. Cleo will teach him. She has a lot of experience being an oracle."

"Is Carmen her god?"

"No, Carmen is something else entirely. Cleo was the oracle of Nemesis—the goddess of…"

"…of retribution. We learned about her in our mythology class."

"Cool," Nash was impressed. "Glad to know at least they're teaching something useful these days. Well, do you know that she is one of the more persistent apparitions of gods in the universe?"

"What does that mean?"

"Most gods are one and done, but some have an essence. A persistence. They come more than once. Nemesis is one of those. She comes every 500 years or so—give or take a decade."

Ray laughed. "Just enough time for humanity to forget previous lessons and needs a goddess to fuck them up."

Nash laughed also, "True. And she is the one to do it." He paused, his eyes lingering a little too long on Ray's handsome face. "Listen, I wanted to say you are totally free here. You can be yourself."

"I am myself," replied Ray uncomfortably. "Not sure what you mean by that."

"I see a lot of myself in you," he said. "Is Calliope your girlfriend?"

"No, she's not my girlfriend."

"You probably should tell her that, because she thinks she is. And now she probably thinks she is going to be your queen."

"My queen! Dude, what are you talking about?"

Nash stood and touched his shoulder, and it wasn't shielded by the force. "I didn't mean to upset you. I want to save you and her from any tragedy."

Ray grabbed Nash's wrist, "You can touch me. I didn't make a shield."

Self-consciously, Nash removed his hand. "I'm sorry."

"It's okay," said Ray. "I didn't mind." He smiled at Nash, "It's okay, really. It was cool I didn't make a shield. You could touch me. I didn't think that was a possibility."

Just then, Dr. Fletcher poked his head in the room. He surveyed the situation with a scrutinous eye. "Everything good?"

"Yeah, no problem," said Ray.

"Jesse, I was hoping you had some time to show me those photos of the divination on Cleo's back. We haven't had time to talk about it."

"Sure," he turned to Ray. "Let me know if you want to talk. Otherwise, we'll start training tomorrow. I was thinking morning for physical training, and in the afternoon, we start working with you and Kendall."

"Sounds like a plan."

Nash joined Fletcher in the hallway outside, and they walked in silence. They took a few turns down some odd-shaped hallways, and then down a shallow set of stairs to another suite of old rooms. Fletcher finally felt they were far enough away from Ray's room to speak.

"What was that about?" asked Fletcher.

"He's lost," said Nash. "I recognize it in his eyes. I was just like that."

Fletcher stopped at a set of double wooden doors and opened them. "Jesse, he's just a teenager. He has a lot on his plate. Please, don't make it more complicated for him."

"I'm not trying to," said Nash. "I'm trying to make it easier for him. That girl, she is bad news I can feel it. She has so much jealousy in her. Can't you see it? Feel it? If anyone can see her for who she is—it is you. That's your father in you."

"For better or worse, she is a goddess. And you don't need to bring up my father, you know that is not something I want people to know. You know it because I trust you, and I want it to stay that way. Got it?"

"Got it, sorry."

"We have to make sure she doesn't go nuclear on us—literally."

"She thinks Ray is her man, and he's not," Nash said angrily.

Fletcher considered his words. "He isn't yours either. Romance is something that the Scholars never dealt with in a successful manner. In fact, they made things worse numerous times."

"Speaking from experience?" smiled Nash.

He sighed, "Don't start."

"Do I have to worry about you, too?"

"Just worry about Ray and Kendall," said Fletcher. "I trust your instincts."

"Thanks." Nash followed the professor into his study. "I texted you the pics. Didn't they come out?" Nash pulled out his phone.

"I saw them, but I was wondering if the originals looked better." Fletcher looked at them again. "Still, no better." He went to an ornately-carved desk that had a wide-screen computer monitor on it. "I'll pull them up." With a few keystrokes the pictures of Cleo's back were in front of them.

"It already started fading when I was able to take the pictures," said Nash.

"Not sure what I'm looking at," Fletcher began, "but I don't think this is *skyborne* anything. Look, these are some kind of appendages, and they are coming down from these clouds."

"I see it," Nash agreed. "What is it?"

"It's a god," replied Fletcher. "I think it is one of the Old Gods."

"The Old Gods?" Nash quizzed. "Like H.P. Lovecraft? That was just fiction."

"Lovecraft was a Scholar, and he worked specifically on the Old Gods."

"Are they like Nemesis?"

"Yes, they are persistent gods. I don't know who this one is, but I believe it is the one that brought down Ray's plane when he was a baby. Think about it, an oracle with a link to an Old God like Nemesis has this divination." His eyes studied the image, "It leads me to believe more and more that Ray is the father of the New Gods."

"You think this Old God tried to kill Ray to stop him from becoming that?"

"Just like the Wire. Ray is a threat to them all if he is able to become the god that humans revere. Then, the Wire will lose all power. And the Old Gods will have to wait who knows how long to become the rulers of Earth again."

"Is there anyone who doesn't want to kill Ray?"

Fletcher shook his head. "I don't know, but I think the reason Nemesis returning is linked to this divination. There are a few books by Vitruvius in the Baltic vaults. Vitruvius was a Scholar who worked with Lovecraft."

"Will you go alone?"

"Do you want to come?" he smiled. "I'd love to take you with me, but you're the only one I trust to keep this place in order while I'm gone."

"Thanks," said Nash.

"I think I will take Calliope with me, though. I have someone I want her to meet. Calliope is her own worst enemy."

"The jealousy?"

"If she doesn't get a handle on it, I'm afraid nothing good will come of it."

"I agree." Nash hesitated before he spoke again. "She's in love with Ray, but he is not in love with her."

"You said that. I know," sighed Fletcher. "I'm not sure I believe that. That's one of the reasons I want to take her with me."

"That will take a little pressure off things around here. Ray needs to get to know Kendall. They barely know each another and they'll be together for who knows how long."

"Any other reasons you don't want her here?" Fletcher studied his acolyte's face.

"No. I can keep him focused better on training."

"Training…" the sentence trailed.

"What's that supposed to mean?"

"I know your type. He is your type."

"Maybe I'm his type, too."

"Like I told you, he has enough to think about."

Nash sighed, "You're right. I will get him trained…with no distractions."

"That's a really good idea," said Fletcher. "Now, I have to go speak to Calliope."

Fletcher found Calliope in her new room. It was similar to Ray's, down to the private bathroom. She was at the desk staring into the laptop that was also given to her. Fletcher cleared his voice to announce his presence.

Calliope looked over at him, "Hey."

"Hey."

"Wanna come in?"

"Yes." Fletcher entered. "So, I have to go on a trip, and I was hoping you would accompany me."

"A trip?" She smiled, "Oh by the way, thanks for the computer. It even has Wi-Fi. Any chance my phone will work again?"

He shook his head, "Not your old one. We can't take the chance of it being traced. I'll get you another one that is secure. But I wanted to ask you to come with me to Europe."

She closed the laptop and laughed. "Now you're screwing with me. You tell me we're literally in protective custody and you want me to go to Europe."

"When you put it that way, I see your point." He pulled up a stool near the desk and sat. "Seriously, I need you to go to Europe with me—specifically Livonia."

"Livonia?" She laughed. "Livonia is just up the expressway."

"Ancient Livonia. How good are you at geography?"

Calliope's face was blank. "I'll take that as a not very good. Okay, ancient Livonia is a place in what is now Estonia and Lithuania." He checked, and her face was still stoic. "How about Sweden? Have you heard of Sweden?"

Calliope's face lit up. "Oh yeah, that's where Robyn is from. Wanna see her video for 'Konichiwa Bitches?'"

Fletcher put his hand on the laptop as she tried to open it. "That won't be necessary. Where we are going is a place in Estonia that would've been located in ancient Livonia—if it still existed. It still does, but not to modern man."

"Is it like this place?" asked Calliope.

"It's a vault, yes. I need to look at some old reference books about something."

"You need to take me with you to look at some old books?" She sized him up, "What else?"

"I want you to meet an old friend of mine named Gunnar. He's a warrior."

"What do you want me to meet him for?"

Fletcher took her hand in his with a certain delicacy. "There is such destructive power here. I don't want you to hurt the people you love, and he can help you."

She pulled her hand away, and a stray ball of light formed on her index finger. "Help me how?"

"Not blow everyone up. Or yourself."

"What if I say no?"

"Let's not go there, okay? I just want you to talk to him, that's it." He smiled, "Come on, how often do you get a free trip to Europe?"

She grinned. "It's not Paris or Barcelona. It's not even Sweden."

"It's really close, trust me."

Calliope sighed. "Well, when are we going? I don't have a passport."

"You don't need one. Can you get your things together, a change of clothes or two—and whatever else you may need? I'll be back in ten minutes, and we'll go."

"Ten minutes? To leave for the airport?"

"You probably won't need an airport ever again." He tapped his eccentric timepiece, "Ten minutes?"

"Ten minutes."

Calliope watched him get up and leave the room. How in hell were they going to get to Europe without aircraft assistance? Where the hell was Livonia? She started to gather items. Is it cold there? Would she need a sweater? Should she look cute?

"Of course, it's cold there," she answered herself. "It's practically the North Pole. And I'm always fucking cute."

It had been nine minutes and thirty-five seconds when Fletcher returned. He wasn't kidding about the ten-minute warning. She hoped he would have been just a little longer because she wanted to look up ancient Livonia on Wikipedia. It sounded like a line of bullshit, but Calliope realized that there was so much more to the world than the thin film she saw on the surface. Ray was indestructible, she could conjure energy, Kendall saw the future, so naturally there was an ancient land called Livonia.

"Ah, good, you're ready." Fletcher was in the doorway and startled her.

Energy balls formed on her fingertips, "You scared me! Don't sneak up on me like that." She held up her fingers, "Now I have these little bombs to get rid of."

"Do they ever fade?" he asked.

"Not really," she replied. "I have never tried, to be honest. They always scare me, so I like to just get rid of them. I just flick them away. I don't want to get burned or blown up."

"Well, hold up your hand and let's watch them for a second."

"What if they start to explode?"

"I don't think they will. I think they're linked to you—to your emotions." He waited. "Breathe and try to relax."

Calliope inhaled deeply and let the air flow. She watched the curious globes of pulsing plasma energy. They were like tiny suns on her fingertips. Then, as theorized by Fletcher, they began to fade until they were gone.

"That was very cool," said Calliope. "I'm going to work on that. Maybe I'll be able to control it. So they are related to my anger and jealousy?"

"Gunnar can help you with that," smiled Fletcher. "You'll like him. He's like a thousand years old, and he had the same problems controlling his emotions."

"Literally?"

"Literally."

"Come at me like you want to kill me," said Nash as he readied himself for the attack.

"When you said physical training in the morning, I thought we were going to lift weights." Ray looked at him uncomfortably. "Maybe some boxing."

"We'll do hand-to-hand eventually." There was a nervous pause, then Nash crouched, "Now come at me."

Ray looked at Nash, he appeared quite dangerous in his white tank top and shorts. Tattoos covered his ripped body, but they couldn't camouflage his leanness or vascularity. Ray dressed for a weight room workout not combat, and sweat started to soak his own tank top and shorts. Nash narrowed his eyes and grinned at the glistening Ray.

"What are you waiting for, Mr. Football Star?"

He fidgeted. "I don't want to hurt you. You know, with my shield."

"Well for some reason, you don't make it with me so that must mean you trust me." Nash smiled. "You won't hurt me, and I will never hurt you."

Ray tried to change the subject as it was making him more nervous, "It's fucking hot in here."

"Excuses, excuses." Nash moved close and gave Ray a gentle shoulder push. "Look, no shield. You won't hurt me. How did you handle those big football players?

"You want to know?" Ray smiled aggressively then rushed his opponent.

In a flash, Nash had Ray on his back—the air knocked out of his lungs. He gasped.

"You may be big, but you're easy to take down. So, what went wrong with that?" Nash stood over Ray and offered his hand to help him off the old mats on the floor. Ray waved him away and went to his knees.

"No, I'm okay."

"You sure?" Nash looked at his downed opponent with concern. "Need to catch your breath?"

Without warning, Ray lashed out and wrapped up Nash's legs. He pulled him down, rotated his grip to his arms, and pinned his chest to the mats with the other. "I was on the wrestling team, too."

Nash laughed. "Obviously."

However, Nash rolled to his back and easily broke Ray's hold. In a flash, Nash had Ray on his back, straddling his chest, pinning Ray's arms with his knees. His hands were around his neck.

"This isn't a high school wrestling match," sweat dripped off his face, splashing on Ray and mixing with his. "This is your life, got it?"

He stared into Ray's eyes, though, daring his opponent to look away. Ray didn't want to. Nash's eyes were penetrating him, exposing him. Finally, he did look away. Nash smiled and let him up. There was slow, sarcastic applause from the doorway. The guys looked to see Poppy standing there.

"You two look like gay porn," she said.

Ray turned bright red. "We were just practicing…"

She laughed. "Relax, I'm just fucking with you."

"I was wondering when you were going to get here," said Nash. "I wasn't sure if you were coming. You're so mysterious these days—vanishing like you did."

"Just mind your own business," she snapped. "I'm here to help Ray train, not to listen to you reprimand me. I have a life other than this place."

Ray pointed as if accusing Poppy of a crime. "I can't fight her. I got 200 pounds on her."

"I can hold my own," she replied.

Poppy glared in Ray's direction. Her eyes washed purple, energy glowed around her upturned palms, and sparkling spears of light launched at Ray. The speed of her attack was shocking, and Ray could only raise his arms helplessly in front of his face. However, it was like his body was one step ahead and the shield protected him as the projectiles vaporized on impact.

"Hey!" shouted Poppy. "They've never disintegrated before!"

Nash laughed. "I guess he doesn't need to train against witches."

Poppy's eyes returned to normal. "Why can you touch him? You were riding him like a daddy bitch without him turning into a lightning bug."

Nash and Ray looked at each other; it was apparent they didn't have an answer. Poppy's eyes turned yellow and she began to summon a different attack from her extensive repertoire. Just as she was about to blast Ray, the entire room shook, and the lights flickered ominously.

"What was that?" Her eyes went back normal.

"What the fuck?" said Nash. The lights dimmed again, "There's something outside."

The room shook again as if a giant were stomping above, and there was a deep, thunderous rumble. This time, the lights went out completely. Poppy generated a luminescent glow to softly light the room so they could see.

"Something's out there," said Ray.

"Maybe it's a bomb," suggested Poppy. "Or the Wire."

"Let's go find out."

The three of them rushed through the labyrinth of halls and stairs to get to the main level. PJ, Cleo, and Carmen were standing in the main tattoo shop, all looked confused about the commotion outside. A deep shockwave shook the *Oracle Tattoo* complex, knocking dust from the ceilings and objects from shelves.

"What the hell is going on?" asked Carmen, her blind eyes darting around.

"An earthquake?" PJ guessed.

"We don't know," answered Nash. "Everyone stay here, I will check it out."

"You can't go out there alone." Ray grabbed his arm. "It's not safe. You don't know what it is. I'm going with you."

"Take him with you," agreed Poppy. "He's fucking bullet-proof."

The two of them went to the door. Ray eased it open, cautiously engaging with the outside world. The street was quiet, but the sky was burdened with heavy clouds. No light was visible, only the gloaming of a storm or approaching twilight.

"Is it a severe thunderstorm?" asked Ray. "Tornado?"

Nash came up behind Ray, "I don't think so." He pointed down the street as a cloud of dust and debris swirled. "What is that?"

Only a few people remained on the street. Most sought shelter from the force of nature approaching from the south. The cloud of debris billowed, rising higher like a column that towered above the buildings. Inside the maelstrom, three luminescent red eyes glared and searched like beacons. Suddenly, Ray glowed and generated a deep golden body halo. It stretched out before them, deflecting the garbage swirling toward them.

"I'm not doing it," said Ray. "My body is doing it on its own."

"Who cares. At least we're not being hit by shrapnel." Nash raised his voice as the wind picked up. "It's moving closer!"

"What is it?" asked Ray.

Cleo, Poppy, PJ, Kendall, and Carmen came out and stood by Nash but behind Ray's protective shield. Each of them simply stared at the growing cloud coming closer. Inside the cloud, the three red eyes darted, scanned, sought. Then, one by one, they settled on the group in front of the tattoo shop.

"Does anyone mind if I run?" asked Poppy.

"You all have powers, I'm screwed," said PJ amidst the growing din of the gale.

"I don't think we can run from it," said Carmen. "I can't see it, but I can smell it. What is it?"

"A giant billowing storm cloud with three red eyes as big as a Mini Cooper." Ray's shield intensified instinctively. "I think if you just stay behind me, it can't hurt us."

Suddenly, inside the cloud and below the eyes, a dark mouth opened. From it, a piercing, debilitating screech shocked them all. Ray's shield stood strong, but the insane sound drilled his ears. Poppy started a spell, but the sound brought the witch to her knees. It moved closer. The sonic attack emboldened the creature.

"It's an Old God," said Nash through the pain. "Fuck!"

"What can we do?" Ray fell to his knees. "I can't fight that sound!"

"Make it stop!" PJ was also on her knees.

Carmen fell as well, shrieking. She covered her ears, unable to protect herself. The creature came closer and closer. The sound shattered car windows along the path between it and the group. Poppy was lying completely prone on the ground, passed out. Ray felt his own will crumble as the sound was unaffected by his shield.

"Poppy! Carmen!" Nash shouted to them, but he was going down, too.

Then Kendall saw that PJ, his dearest friend, had become motionless. A trickle of blood came from her left ear, pooling and dripping off her chin.

"PJ!" The others looked. "We have to help her!"

Kendall covered his ears; the sound was too intense. Ray fought the attack, but he was being weakened as well. He was indestructible physically, but sonically he was vulnerable. Somehow the Old God knew it. Ray tried to concentrate, pushing his shield outward, creating intimidating glowing spears. He pushed them outward towards the monster. One went through a red eye. The Old God's voice dropped in intensity, convoking pain. There were only two eyes open now. It retreated down the street, but didn't seem to be giving up. The reprieve allowed Kendall, Poppy, and Carmen to recover a little. But PJ was still down, blood streaming down her face.

Kendall rushed to her, scooping her limp body into his arms. "PJ! PJ! Wake up!" He looked at the others, helpless. "Please, what do we do?"

Carmen knelt by them and placed a hand on PJ's forehead. She was unconscious and still bleeding. Then Carmen opened her eyes, they were not her usual blind orbs, instead a pinpoint of intense deep light rose in her dark pupils. A halo of white radiance circled them.

Carmen spoke, but it was not her voice: "She's nearly dead."

"No!" Kendall screamed, anguished, helpless. "Save her!"

Ray pushed harder with a second spear of his energy. He had to save them, protect them. The creature, however, anticipated it, and it only pierced a part of its cloud body harmlessly. Nash went to Carmen who knelt over PJ's limp body. The blood was still streaming, and now it was coming from both ears. This was going be how they all died if they couldn't stop the Old God.

Then, he saw Carmen's eyes. Carmen was not in there. It was Nemesis.

"I can save her," Carmen's mouth spoke with Nemesis' voice.

"Do it," Nash grabbed Carmen's hand. "I won't mention this. Just save her."

"It's time, don't worry." The smile was Nemesis. "I am here."

Carmen stood and faced the Old God. It was preparing a renewed attack, but now hesitated. The two good eyes locked onto Carmen, and the sound decreased in decibels. Ray's shield contracted back to him, becoming thick and nearly opaque.

Carmen side-stepped the shield in order to have a clear view of the creature.

"Methoraloth, back down or die." Carmen began to float on a ribbon of pink luminescent light coming from the very air itself. "You know me."

The mouth shut completely, silencing the attack. Relief was like a bomb going off around them. They could breathe again, their ears could hear again through a residual tinnitus. Poppy woke. Their sight cleared. Methoraloth opened its mouth and one booming word erupted: "Him."

"You cannot have him," she replied. "Retreat or die."

Methoraloth growled and laughed. "Tiny goddess."

Carmen rose higher on the Veil. The bloodstream of the universe. She was the Hammer. She was the arm. The ribbon of light streamed through her body then up through her shoulders, and finally out through her extended arms. Methoraloth hesitated.

With no effort, the ribbons ejaculated from Carmen's hands. Each found a remaining red eye. Methoraloth howled. The ungodly blast broke any remaining windows on the street. The cars buckled on top of the writhing pavement. Ray's shield protected them as shrapnel rained down around them. The bloodstream of the universe, the arm, the weapon, the Hammer struck. Methoraloth melted into his own cloud and the gales he brought took him away. Carmen descended on the Veil, head lowered and calm.

She turned her blind eyes towards PJ and went to her. "She will die if I don't save her."

"What can you do?" Tears poured down Kendall's face. "She is my best friend, please…"

"Dear oracle, I can save her, but I have to take her away." She knelt, placing both her hands on PJ's chest. "I cannot guarantee she will survive Methoraloth's attack, but she will certainly die if I leave her here."

The Veil surged in Carmen, consuming them both in the

bloodstream. It flowed away from the earth and into the sky, taking them with it, molecule by molecule. And as quickly as it began, they were gone.

"This is an interesting building," said Calliope as Fletcher escorted her out of an ancient brick tunnel beneath an equally ancient fort.

"Welcome to Livonia," he smiled, "and not the one in Michigan."

"Very funny."

"What you are walking through, or under, is the home of the Knights of the Teutonic Order."

"Who were they?"

"Who *are* they," he corrected. "There are a few of them left."

"Are they like you?"

"No, I am a Scholar and I'm here to do some work in the Scholar Library here. Oracle Tattoo is also a Scholar Library."

"The tattoo shop? That's a library?"

"Do not let the size of that building fool you, it can be as big as all of this—or smaller than a dog house."

"That makes no sense, professor." She marveled as they walked up some stone stairs and into a great hall. "This is incredible."

Before their eyes, the polished marble floors stretched to 40-foot windows with a view of the Baltic Sea. Showcases with artifacts were on the floor; paintings and scrolls hung on the stone walls. There were three men standing at various entrances, each dressed in dark suits and glasses.

"Those are Knights of the Teutonic Order," Fletcher's voice was a whisper, but it carried in the building. "They are quite formidable."

"I thought they'd be in armor, not Calvin Klein."

Fletcher stopped her. "Oh, those are Dior suits. Calvin Klein is basic." He grinned, "And those suits are better than armor, they're bulletproof, fireproof, bombproof. Literally hell-proof."

At the far end of the cavernous space, two more Knights appeared. They were walking behind a regal blonde woman in a fitted navy suit. Something in the confident way she strode, like the seas would part if she wished it so, made Calliope a bit nervous. Her heels clicked on the stone in cadence.

As she got closer to Fletcher, she smiled. "I wondered when I would see you again, Phineas."

Fletcher took her extended hand and gave it soft kiss, "My dear, Astrid. It is always an event to see you."

Astrid glanced at Calliope and saw the remnant of a subtle eye roll. "He can be so full of it. You must be Calliope."

"I am," Calliope made an awkward curtsey.

"No need for anything like that," said Astrid. "I'm only a scholar like Dr. Fletcher here."

"Don't let her fool you, Dr. Astrid Petersen is the president of the Scholars."

"Do you mind if I ask how old you are?" asked Calliope.

"Of course not, I'm 155."

Calliope turned to Fletcher. "I so need to be a scholar."

"Well you can't, you're a god," Fletcher said curtly. He turned to Dr. Petersen, "I need to do some reading on the Old Gods from Vitruvius."

"Any reason in particular?" asked Petersen.

"No, not really. Just a divination that was hard to interpret."

"Who had the divination? Cleo?"

Fletcher nodded. "I just wanted to clear a few possibilities off the table."

Then, one of the Knights leaned over and whispered something to Astrid. Her face no longer smiled. "We just got news of an attack at your home."

"What do you mean?" Fletcher asked, looking at Calliope who was visibly concerned. He watched as a few orbs collected on her fingernails. "Let's stay calm until we can find out what happened. I'm sure everything is okay."

Petersen, as well as the Knights, noticed the display of power. "Yes, let's not have an accident here. Come on, there is a conference room on the second floor where we can go." Petersen leaned to one of her companions, "Can you see if Dr. Allende can meet us and debrief us?" He nodded and left. "Follow me, please."

Fletcher and Calliope dropped in behind them as they went back the way they came. A sudden new flurry of activity infected the outpost. More people hurried around, going to destinations with serious expressions on their faces. A few more knights appeared as well and took positions near some of the larger windows.

They entered the conference room, which overlooked the Baltic Sea. There was a long mahogany table with enough seats for twenty. However, they were the only ones in the room. Just behind them, another Scholar entered. He was distinguished with thick silver hair and a large beard of equal luster.

"Phineas, what a pleasure to see you again. Sorry that we have to share bad news with you."

"Bad news? Wait, what about this attack Astrid told us about."

He took a remote off the table and pressed a few buttons. A wide-screen monitor hanging on the wall blinked to life. On it, there was a newsfeed from the United States and the headline was about a tornado that ripped through downtown Detroit.

"I take it, it wasn't a tornado," commented Fletcher.

"To be honest, we don't know. We looked at Doppler radar of the city and there was no supercell in the area. It was just cloudy from what we can tell. However, there were exploded windows all along the street outside your tattoo studio."

"We were cloaked. The Wire never found us. And now we think that an Old God found us?"

"Is anyone hurt?" asked Calliope.

Petersen and Allende exchanged pensive glances. "Intelligence regarding the incident is still sketchy," he said. "We just don't know."

"We have to go back," said Calliope. "What if Ray is hurt?"

"Ray isn't the one who would get hurt," quipped Fletcher. "There is no other information you can tell us?"

Allende shook his head. "I'm afraid not. There are no casualties reported if that is any consolation."

"Maybe we should go back," said Fletcher. "Perhaps, I can take the books back with me."

"Books can't leave the vault, you know that, Phineas." Petersen looked out the window. "Who did you leave in charge? Nash?"

"Yes, he's very capable."

"We'll send someone over to look in on things," replied Petersen. "You should stay here and do your work."

"No, we should go back," said Calliope. Her fingers were coated in plasma balls, "Ray may be hurt."

"I told you he isn't the one that will get hurt."

"Then let's go back and check on the others."

Astrid Petersen interrupted, "Trust us, Calliope, we'll make sure everyone is safe and accounted for."

Fletcher agreed, "They can handle it. You will tell us when you have more news, right?"

"Of course," said Allende. "Go do your research."

Fletcher nodded. "Come on, Calliope. I'll show you the vaults. They are quite impressive."

They walked together in silence for more than 20 minutes. They passed through the massive complex and out onto the island itself, which was covered in pebbles, driftwood, and lichen. To Calliope, this didn't seem like an appropriate way to a vault. The vaults of the tattoo shop were a labyrinth. She went a little further, but ultimately had to pause.

"Excuse me, but this doesn't seem like we are going in the right direction," said Calliope.

Fletcher paused and took in the grey sky. "It's because we're not."

"Where are we going then?"

"Not to the vaults because the books aren't there. Astrid is a very shady person to say the least. Allende is just as bad. They are political players at all this. They don't love scholarship they love the power they have because of it."

"Then where are we going?"

"We're going to see Gunnar. At least we can fulfill that part of the mission, right?"

"I suppose so." Calliope followed as Fletcher led the way towards a low set of buildings on the water's edge. "What's so special about this guy?"

"He reminds me of you."

"Is that good or bad?"

Fletcher didn't answer. He walked down a wooden dock that led to an ancient structure composed of enormous fieldstones left behind by the glaciers. It appeared to be an old fort designed to protect from naval attacks.

"Phineas Fletcher!" The voice boomed from above. "I didn't expect you so early. I shall be down momentarily."

"He seems very happy," commented Calliope.

"He is now. It took a while."

"What happened?"

"That's his story to tell you," said Fletcher. Just then the heavy door opened. "Gunnar, it's so good to see you."

Calliope took in Gunnar. He was older to be sure, but insanely handsome to her. Bright blue eyes, greying beard that was still mostly auburn, a tight blue thermal shirt revealed his fit body.

Gunner took Fletcher into an aggressive hug. "Good to see you! Good to see you!" He pulled back. "How is your little family back in the U.S.?"

"They are fine, very eventful lately, however."

Calliope looked at Fletcher, "Family?"

"He means Cleo and Jesse. And now the rest of you." He smiled. "This is Calliope."

Gunnar reached out his hand and took hers. He was surprisingly gentle with his rough, calloused work hands. "Lovely to meet you."

"Can we go inside?" asked Fletcher. "I'm not very comfortable with Astrid Petersen in charge of things right now."

"Absolutely, then you can update me." Gunnar smiled at Calliope, "I try to stay out of the drama, and I'm happily ignorant."

"I wish I could say the same," she said.

They went inside and closed the door.

Ray sighed. He wiped the sweat from his face—and the blood from his broken eyebrow. He looked in the small mirror in his room to check the damage. It was the first time in his life he'd seen his own blood. Ray never thought of the possibility before but it didn't scare him. He was fascinated that someone on this planet was able to draw blood with a punch.

"Wow, what happened to you?" asked Kendall from the doorway. "Do I even want to know?"

"Yeah, you should know." Ray turned around, "Jesse handed me my hat."

"Nah, he beat your ass." Kendall laughed. He had a small dinner plate with a tiny cake on it. "I made this for you."

"What is it?" asked Ray, walking towards him.

"It's your birthday cake, dork." Kendall offered it up for inspection, "There is actually a well-equipped kitchen here. I went exploring and decided you needed a birthday cake."

"Birthday, huh? I totally forgot."

"I think everyone did, but I didn't." Kendall walked past him and put the cake on the desk. "I'm a shitty baker, just so you know. And I figure it's my job to know all about you so I stalked you. Happy 18th. You're a man now."

Ray laughed. "I don't feel like much of a man. Look at my face."

"You're still pretty," said Kendall and Ray blushed. "Seriously, are you going to tell me how Jesse was able to do that to your face?"

"Yeah, we were sparring."

"Come on, the truth. I can tell, remember?"

The reminder made Ray a little more uncomfortable. "I forgot about that. You don't read minds, do you?"

"I don't read minds," he replied. "But you can trust me. We are going to be together a long time."

"Nash can touch me."

"Like your skin?"

Ray nodded. "He can touch me. I don't produce a shield around him."

"Wow, that's incredible. I wonder why?"

"It made me nervous, for sure." Ray walked over to check out the cake, "This isn't too bad. 'Happy B-day.'"

"It's a small cake, and I couldn't write birthday."

"I appreciate it, really." Ray put a finger in the frosting and licked it. "This is really good. When is your birthday?"

"I turned 18 back in February. I'm the guy in my group of friends who makes sure everyone gets a little something and a card."

"It's weird that we're hanging out here and not back in school," said Ray. "Wonder why?"

"You know why, you aren't that much of a naïve boy scout." Kendall walked over and also took a swipe of frosting. "I'm an out gay guy, and you are Mr. All-American dream…"

"…since I was 17…"

"…don't matter if I step on the scene…"

"…or sneak away to the Philippines…"

Kendall laughed, "OMG, are we sharing Britney lyrics?"

Ray laughed too. "I love Britney."

"Do you mind if I ask you a personal question?" asked Kendall.

Ray shrugged. "I don't care."

"Have you ever kissed a guy?"

It wasn't the kind of question he was expecting. "I thought you were going to ask about my birthday or something."

"Knowing if you kissed a guy is far more interesting."

"Why do you want to know that?" Ray fidgeted.

"I just get a vibe from you…and not this oracle shit…like a real *vibe*, you know?" Kendall stood next to Ray, "Forget I asked that. Sorry. That's personal."

"No, it's okay. I haven't, to be honest with you." He hesitated. "Not that I haven't thought about it. I think everyone has thought about it."

"Kissing a dude?"

Ray laughed nervously, "I mean a dude thinking that about another dude. Or a girl thinking what it would be like to kiss a girl."

"I guess I can relate to that," said Kendall. "PJ is a lesbian. God, I hope she's okay—wherever she is. I'm trying not to think about it."

"Me, too." Ray hung his head, "I should have been able to protect her. I should have been able to stop that thing. How did it get stopped?"

"I was in so much pain I don't remember a thing."

"Carmen is gone, too." Ray closed his eyes and remembered, "There was like all this noise and I went down. I glanced up and saw a bunch of weird light hitting the creature, but I couldn't keep my eyes open."

"I can't remember, really." Kendall moved intimately close to Ray. "Do you mind if I try something?"

Ray inched back, "Like what?"

"I want to see if I can touch you."

Before Ray could answer yes or no, Kendall reached out and softly placed his hand on his chest. There was no shield, only hot skin with a lingering dew of perspiration. The pulse just beneath separated only by millimeters of flesh from Kendall's own eager palm.

"You can touch me." Ray was shocked and pulled away.

"Wait, it's okay. There is nothing wrong with us touching each other." He looked Ray dead in his eyes. "I like touching you."

"Don't you get it?" He plunged his hand into the cake and took a fistful. "If you can touch me, and Jesse can touch me, what if there are others who can touch me. But will want to kill me?" He threw the cake and hit Kendall in the cheek. "Like that."

"I get it." Kendall took a handful of cake and threw it at Ray. "If someone can touch you they can hurt you. Let me be the first to tell you, it's not the ones who can touch you and hurt you—it's the fuckers that can't or won't touch you who can do the most damage."

Ray threw another handful of cake and laughed uncontrollably. Kendall scooped up remnant frosting and tossed it at Ray; they both were hysterical. Each flung bits of cake at each other until they could find no more, then nearly collapsed on one another with disabling laughter. At last they stopped and simply stood looking at each other with faces covered with frosting and cake.

Ray took Kendall's hand and put it on his chest. "Can I ask you a question?"

The move surprised Kendall, but he wasn't going to say a damn word. "Yeah, you can trust me."

"What's it like…" he hesitated, "…to be kissed by another guy?"

Kendall opened his mouth to reply, but stopped. He looked into Ray's eyes and saw genuine vulnerability, a longing for wisdom. A part of Kendall wanted to just dive in and show him what that kiss would feel like, but another part reminded him this was trust.

Instead of answering, Kendall turned back to the cake plate and found a lone dollop of remaining frosting. He scooped it onto his index finger. Kendall raised his hand, finger with frosting pointing upward. Then he looked into Ray's eyes—hard. Kendall smeared the frosting across Ray's lips.

"It tastes like frosting."

Kendall's pink tongue found one corner of Ray's mouth. The stubble of Ray's chin pricked Kendall's tongue as it collected the frosting lingering on his lips. He continued across Ray's mouth, a lazy swirl, and paused once he reached the center. Kendall pursed his lips and found Ray's equally eager mouth ready to kiss back.

"God it does taste like frosting." Ray was savagely kissing Kendall. "Fuck."

"Happy Birthday, Ray."

EPIS💠DE EIGHT

The Pierian Spring

Nemesis stood above PJ and Carmen, who were in soft beds in front of her. Her long black hair was a cascade over her cobalt blue war leather. They were just girls; they shouldn't be fighting death like this. She touched their heads. Perhaps, she would have to speak to Death himself and strike a deal. That could wait, however.

"My lady," a young woman with dark ebony skin and flowers circling her short hair approached, "there is still no change in them."

"Keep a close eye, please." Nemesis sighed, "If the Pierian Spring cannot help them, then they may be the first casualties of the New Gods."

Nemesis walked to the edge of the large pool ringed with heavy stones. She sat down and peered over into the limpid water. There were no ripples, no bubbles, just her own reflection that quivered ever so slightly. She needed counsel. Nemesis focused on reaching Cleo. Or Dione. Or whatever name she adopted upon her god's departure.

Hear me.

Nemesis lay down on the stones. Her hand drifted until it touched the magic waters of the Pierian Spring. It was cool, filling her with calm. Nemesis' mind telegraphed outward through the Veil, searching for her oracle.

I hear you.

Her mind touched Cleo's. It was familiar, comfortable, soothing.

I have missed you, my oracle.

I have missed you, my goddess.

Nemesis concentrated. She could not get caught in emotions when she needed clear divination. It would be so easy, though, to just give in to the emotions and wipe the world clean. Retribution was a drug. Carmen was her vessel. Nemesis did not have a body of her own.

What do you see, my oracle? Guide me. Counsel me.

Two souls are with you. One is claimed already by Pluto. He will come for her.

Who?

He will make you choose.

The connection severed. Nemesis sat up on the stone ledge and looked over at the two young women resting in limbo. They weren't young women; they were both children. Pluto would indeed make her choose. After all, she was the goddess of retribution, balance, payments. She would be required to measure them against one another then choose one to send beyond to Pluto. She did not want to deal with Pluto, but sooner or later it would have to happen. Nemesis had hoped for later than sooner, but the water of the Pierian Spring began to bubble.

"Looks like it will be sooner..." Nemesis whispered to herself as the water foamed and rippled.

Then from beneath the waters, like a stoic ancient sculpture of an overly muscled Michelangelo sculpture, the white-bearded god, Pluto, rose. The water drained from his broad shoulders, immense chest, defined abdominals, square hips, and thick striated thighs as he emerged. He was not shy of his form.

"Nemesis," he said.

"Pluto," she replied. "I have expected you."

"I'm sure your oracle divined it for you. My oracle did as well and that is how I located you here. It was wise to bring the mortals to the spring."

"I had to spare them if I could," she said.

"That is unlike you. What is different? Usually, there is objective deliverance from the goddess of retribution."

"This is not a normal time," she said. "This time, the *newborne* gods are led by someone as formidable as your brother Zeus. Even more so…he is indestructible."

"Every god has a weakness," said Pluto.

He stepped out of the water and onto the stones. With measured gaze, he considered the two young women prone near the magical waters. He went to them and placed his large palms on each of their foreheads. Then, Pluto closed his eyes. He let their souls mingle with his energy, tasting them as only he could.

Nemesis watched. It was not often she felt helpless as a god, but it was always so in Pluto's presence. No god had greater empathy for mortals as he. The myths and stories about the wrathful god of the underworld were manufactured by humans and could not be further from reality.

Finally, he opened his eyes. "Either one of these children is ready to travel with me. But I will not take both. You will need to decide."

Nemesis sighed, "My oracle told me as much."

"My oracle reached out to me to come personally to escort the chosen one."

"Why?"

"This one," he glanced down at Carmen, "she is the Hammer of the Veil. It has been so very long since a mortal was able to serve the Veil fully. She does." He removed his hands from the girls and leveled his blue eyes at Nemesis, "she is also your vessel. Without her, you cannot be in the mortal world. You need her."

"I must be in the world at this time, great Pluto. I was called to return for some reason."

"Your oracle has no divination for you?"

She shook her head, "Unfortunately, I have not been able to consult her properly. I've only recently been able to emerge. The girl's will is quite strong and she can suppress me. I was awoken when she entered the Veil and was about to die. I possessed her and wielded the Hammer to save her."

"Who sent her into the Veil?"

Nemesis swallowed hard. She could not lie to Pluto. "Phineas."

There was no immediate answer from the god, only a barely audible sigh. "Phineas."

Nemesis nodded, "It's true."

Pluto again pierced her with his gaze, "Did he have a reason to do that?"

"I…" she hesitated. "One of my priestesses sent him a *khonshu* from my temple."

"How did your priestess know to send him a token?" He turned back to Carmen, "It doesn't matter, Nemesis. You arranged for the token to be sent to Phineas. No sense in denying it. Fate was dictating the context."

"Forgive me."

"You still love him, don't you?"

Nemesis only nodded.

"Again, no matter for me. I have to attend to these two at the moment. Whom do you choose?"

Nemesis weighed her choice. For millennia she has been a god, but this decision was more difficult than it should be. The mortal girl, PJ, for whom she only knew for a brief time, seemed to be quite important to Phineas. And Phineas was important to her. He looked upon her like a daughter. Would it be wrong to send this girl to Hades?

Carmen, however, was critical to Nemesis and her return to the mortal world. She was her vessel. Not just any person can be a vessel, there were criteria. The host had to be female, only a female was strong enough to host a god such as Nemesis. There was no way to know how long until another suitable vessel would emerge that the Veil would allow her to inhabit. Then there was the Veil itself: Carmen was the very hand of universe.

"Take the girl," said Nemesis.

"Which one?" replied Pluto. "They are both children."

"That one, the girl named PJ." Nemesis pointed at her. "Carmen is indispensable."

"Only because she is your vessel to the mortal world?"

Angrily, Nemesis turned. "Do not go there, Pluto. The one you are taking is very important to Phineas. I don't think he will forgive this choice. For either of us."

"He will never know."

With that Pluto stood. He seemed even larger than before as he approached the girls. Then he raised his hand over PJ and her body rose. Effortlessly, Pluto scooped her into his muscular arms and turned towards the Pierian Spring. Nemesis watched as he waded into the water and slowly descended into the netherworld.

For many moments, Nemesis watched the water. It was still, motionless, dark. What had she done? Did she make a selfish decision? She was the god of retribution and equality. Would she now be able to make judgements by putting herself first? There was no other choice.

"You seem troubled," said a voice from behind.

Nemesis turned to see Carmen sitting up, her blind eyes unfocused yet gazing in her direction. She knew the girl could "see" her though; the Veil was her eyes now. They were not in the mortal world. They were in the grotto of the Pierian Spring—a solemn, holy place for the persistent gods such as Nemesis and Pluto.

"You didn't expect me to wake," said Carmen.

"I did not," replied Nemesis. "I'm glad to see it."

Thin tendrils of pink Veil energy twined about Carmen. "Are you?" She looked at the empty bed next to her, "Where is PJ?"

Nemesis hesitated. "Pluto has claimed her."

"Pluto? The former planet?"

"No, the god of the Underworld," said Nemesis.

"I don't understand, who is Pluto? Satan is the god of the Underworld. Hell."

"Hell is a myth. Satan is a lie. There was never a fallen angel. It was all made up by the Wire to control human beings."

"I don't understand," the ribbons twined even more. "You are lying."

"I can't expect you to understand, but you will. I know you can feel the universe in your veins."

Carmen paused. "Wait, I remember your voice. It was in the shadows where Professor Fletcher sent me."

Nemesis nodded. "I saved you. You weren't ready to engage the Veil full on. He should have never sent you into it. I heard your call and came to your rescue."

"You have been in my head. I know your voice. You have been in my body. For how long? How long have you been controlling me?"

"It isn't like that," said Nemesis. "You are my vessel. I am the goddess Nemesis. I am the goddess of retribution."

"If you are a goddess, then why do you need my body?"

"There is much work to do, and we need each other."

"What do you need me for if you're a god?"

"The mortal world, for me requires a vessel, and you are the Veil's arm in the world. Together we can protect the new gods from being killed in their very cribs by the Wire."

"This Wire you keep talking about, what is that?"

"Phineas didn't tell you? It is a group of very cruel mortals who destroy gods before they can rise and provide hope for the world."

Carmen laughed, "I'm sorry. Gods provide hope for this world? What have gods ever done for anyone but themselves? I heard Fletcher saying all that shit. And it is all just shit. Look at me. I'm fucking blind. I'm poor. I'm Latina, and I'm a woman. I have been abused by men, white men, since I was a child. There is no God. They didn't help me. Where was He when I needed Him?"

"The God you are thinking of doesn't exist. He never existed. He was created centuries ago, carefully, by the Wire. They created all the religious myths to control human beings. Because when there is a true god to bring all people together, man cannot control other men."

"So, this Wire kills gods before they can become gods so they can keep control over the world?"

Nemesis nodded. "You have seen it. I know what you know. I have experienced the Wire's attacks on you and your friends. I rescued you from the attack from the Old Gods outside the tattoo shop."

"The Old Gods?" The ribbons rose around Carmen. "More lies? Who are the Old Gods? How many are there?"

"You may not remember. I took control when the attack happened, to save all of you."

"I'm fucking blind, bitch. I didn't see anything."

"You heard the sonic attack. The Old Gods are even older than I am. Or Pluto. Or any of the other persistent gods. The earth has always been a god-friendly place. At one time, the Old Gods co-existed with the rise and fall of the other gods, but they lost control when the gods of Olympus rose. That was the golden age of gods. They drove the Old Gods under. They killed many of them. And the Old Gods have been waiting for a time when there were no gods to reassert themselves. They have been waiting as the Wire kills the *newbornes* until they decide they are ready to take over the earth."

"This is so confusing," said Carmen. "You are lying. You are messing with my mind. You just want my body to control me. You want to control the Veil."

"The Veil is the one thing that binds all gods, people, and things together," said Nemesis. "It's true that the power of the Veil can be beneficial. But the Veil is seductive and will bend to the emotional will of the Hammer. You."

"Are you saying I will misuse the power?"

Nemesis shook her head, realizing the Veil was rising on Carmen's mistrust and anxiety. "Not at all. I have been the Hammer before, and I know how the bloodstream of the universe exerts its influence."

"Does that mean I am the new god of retribution?" smiled Carmen. "Maybe I am the one to use its power."

"You need to use the Veil to protect the new gods from the Wire. Ray does not need to be protected. He is indestructible. He is destined to be the one god, the father that unites this earth for peace."

"I know Ray, and he's a dumb jock."

"You do know him, that's true. Then you know him to be kind and benevolent. He was protecting all of you from an attack from one of the Old Gods. He wasn't ready, though. He would have survived, but the rest of you would have died. I saved you. Unfortunately, I could not save your friend."

"I still don't believe you." The ribbons of the Veil agitated, swelled, swirled, elongated. Thick, almost liquid fog dripped and pooled from Carmen's body. "I think you are the problem."

The pink tendrils darkened to a thick, savage purple. They struck out like cobra tongues and bound Nemesis tightly. Nemesis' eyes washed silver as her godly powers were called upon. She began to struggle against the Veil, rising, but the ribbons rose with her.

"This is not the way," raged Nemesis. "You do not want me as your enemy."

"I'm not afraid of you." Carmen manipulated the Veil, moving Nemesis over the waters of the Pierian Spring. "I will be a better you."

The Veil consumed Nemesis, encapsulating her in a cocoon of undulating energy. The blood of the universe obeyed. Then, Nemesis was plunged beneath the waters of the magical spring. For many minutes, Carmen concentrated on manipulating the Veil.

Send her away. Send her far, far away. Do not let her get in my way. No escape.

Calliope leaned on the old bricks of the fort and watched the low sun over the Baltic. It was a dim orange blob of sherbet melting in the cotton candy-colored sky. The wind came off the water, moving her hair in delicate wisps that tickled her ears and neck. There was salt in the air.

Approaching from behind, Gunnar leaned on the wall next to her. "Beautiful, isn't it? Funny, too."

"Funny?" She glanced at him. "How so?"

"It's nearly midnight."

"I was wondering when this day was going to end," she said. "The professor said he would be back."

"He would pick the long, midnight sun days to say he'd be back by sundown." Gunnar laughed. "He is the king of twisting words and non-commitment."

"I thought he was your friend?"

"He used to be a great friend..." Gunnar's words trailed. "Now, I just pretend. He is someone to keep close, to keep up an illusion of friendship."

She looked at him. "Why are you telling me this? We don't know each other. Aren't you afraid I will tell him?"

"No, you won't tell him," he said. "I think I've gotten to know you for the short time we have been together. You already know he isn't coming back. He left you here."

The truth simmered in her mind. She was thinking it, but Calliope hoped it wasn't true.

"You are not part of his plan with this kid Ray." She was

silent as he spoke. "He's casting his bets with him. He thinks that kid is the next coming, literally."

"What do you think that means?"

"It means the rest of you are his bit players," said Gunnar. "Like me, you get to be a bit player in his drama."

"You realize now you have to tell me everything," she smiled.

"I don't think I do," he said. Then he pointed at three crows that had landed on the wall facing the water. "I take it they belong to you."

Calliope looked at the birds. Their black eyes flickered rather than blinked; their heads moved in jerky sudden jolts.

"My oracles," she mumbled. "I can't even get a human oracle."

"Humans are overrated," said Gunnar. "Humans fuck everything up." He pointed at the birds, "Do you think they need to give you a message?"

The birds hopped down onto the rock and wooden deck, fidgeting with their wings and beaks, sniping at each other. Squawking like gossiping old women. Tearing at each other's feathers. Two emerged as dominant and began to peck, peck, peck at the weaker one. It shrieked as feathers and flesh were plucked out. Savagely, they attacked until it was dead, its guts spilled on the stone.

Calliope walked to the scene and looked over at the intestines and blood. Gunnar joined her. She puzzled over the configuration, there wasn't anything jumping out at her. Then she looked at Gunnar.

"What do you see?" she asked.

He sighed. "That's a good question. I'm not sure what I see will make any sense to you. You are the god."

"I don't see anything," she sighed. "It looks like a pile of… of guts."

"Look closer," urged Gunnar.

"Can you read divinations?"

"Somewhat. It's not difficult." He pressed her, "Now what do you see?"

She examined the entrails that twisted and twined around a bloody, bulbous lump of tissue. "It kinda looks like an octopus or squid. That looks like a head," she pointed, "and the guts trailing out look like tentacles, don't you think?"

"That's what I see, too," said Gunnar. "Come with me."

As they stood, the two live crows covered their dead sibling with their wings. He reconstituted beneath their cover and all three flew away. Gunnar walked back to the edge of the fortress wall and peered out over the dark Baltic Sea. The water was now black and menacing.

"What do you see when you look out at the water?" he asked.

Calliope was unsure of what he meant. "Nothing, it's just water. I can't see anything it is so black."

"That great blackness is not the water," he said. "That is the blackness of the Old Ones. The Old Gods. The rightful gods of this small blue world."

She looked again. "I still don't see it." Then, she turned and considered Gunnar. "Who are you and how do you know so much about this stuff?"

He laughed. "I am a product of the gods."

"You're a god?"

"No, not like that." He pointed to the water, "Out there, in the ocean, is where the real god is. I am casting my lot with him, not you new gods. No offense. You are just children. You will be undone by human emotions and ego."

"Why are you saying these things?" Upon her fingertips, plasma balls formed and sparked. Her trust radar went off. Men couldn't be trusted.

"Put away your weaponry, I have no fight with you."

The energy faded. "Who do you have beef with?"

"Beef?"

"A problem. Who do you have a problem with?"

He sighed as if he was making a big internal decision. "You don't know Phineas like I do. The *real* Phineas."

"Tell me."

"You have to meet someone first, and then perhaps…"

"Who?"

"Just look, out there in the water."

Gunnar closed his eyes and held out his right hand. He gripped an unseen object. Then suddenly, a weapon formed. It was a long spear, but the tip was wide and elaborately etched. To Calliope it resembled a machete atop a long pole.

"What's that?"

"It's my *atgeir*. The bitter reminder of my curse."

The water churned, but there were no bubbles for whatever was coming was pushing deep water towards the surface from the inky abyss. The grey-black mass surfaced, so large it appeared to move in slow motion. Time seemed to push at it, withstand the coming, but it could not be held beneath the waves. Calliope and Gunnar were insects as the creature rose higher and higher in the air. Water cascaded down its cephalopod head, a dome in which two immense eyes were embedded. Large as naval vessels, black and shiny, dripping, sodden.

Calliope wanted to run, her instinct to protect herself caused the formation of plasma balls of a size and intensity she'd never been able to conjure before to form and engulf her hands. They pulled away from her body and hovered, igniting the sky with brilliant white light.

Impressive.

The voice was in her head.

Who said that?

I did. The god that is before you.

"Gunnar, can you hear that? This monster is in my head."

"He is not a monster, dear child." Gunnar smiled. "This is what a god looks like."

Child who commands the Sun. I come to you with a proposal.

"He says he wants to propose something," said Calliope.

"I can hear him, too." Gunnar lowered his atgeir. "I advise you to listen."

You have great power, starborne. And the time for you is just beginning.

I have returned to claim my rightful place as the god of this world. I will wipe this planet clean—to start again. No more god cycles. You and I, great goddess of humans, shall be my bride. My partner. Together, we will command this world.

I don't even know your name.

I am the Old God, the ancient one who needs no name. I only am. My existence is my definition. I have no need for a mouth to speak. I communicate with you through the Veil. The bloodstream of the universe. It flows in both of us. Two powerful gods.

The orbs of deadly sparking plasma still hovered in the air between them.

Young goddess, use your gift to destroy the humans who wish to destroy us. Humans are beneath us. They will murder you if they can. They fear us. I will not let them kill you. I will place you where you belong on the highest mountain to rule over them.

Then, there was a pause. The voice faded in her mind.

"Gunnar, what do I do? I think I made him angry. He stopped talking."

"The Old One is waiting for a response. I would not keep him waiting."

Calliope swallowed hard. "I'm scared. We can't even get out of this damn place. Dr. Fletcher stranded us here."

Silence, now. The Old One's voice returned.

For too long you have lived among the common roaches of humankind. A war is coming. New gods versus Old. Many will die on both sides. But the victors will reign forever. Human gods will betray you for they will fear you. No god has commanded the sun as you do now. As my compatriot, your place at my side is guaranteed. You will be a queen. Forever.

"What do I do, Gunnar?"

"You say yes."

Yes.

Before she even considered saying it, Calliope thought it. The Old Nameless God heard her. Then he sank below the waves and disappeared.

"What just happened?"

Gunnar smiled, "You just made yourself Queen." He winked at her. "Now, to get us out of this place forever."

She watched him as he walked towards the stairs and her energy faded. "Where are you going?"

"Back to the outpost to get our ticket to freedom. An aperture."

"Where is the goddess Nemesis?" Asked one of the Pierian Spring attendants as she returned. She noticed Carmen standing, "Dear girl! Are you okay? You are alive!"

"I *am* alive," replied Carmen.

Three more attendants returned.

"Sisters!" said the first. "Behold the miracle of the Spring. Our guest has revived."

"Who are you four?" asked Carmen.

"We are the guardians of the Pierian Spring," said one who appeared to be older. "To drink or bathe in the spring is akin to being kissed by the gods. Truth and clarity are its gifts."

"What is your name and are you in charge here?"

"My name is Lucina," said the one who spoke before. She was dark-skinned, flawless, with her hair hidden by a pristine white dhuku. "These are my sisters, Euippe, Polyxo, and Haemonia. We are the attendants."

Each of the also wore white dhukus, and they were equal in beauty to their sister.

Euippe took a step closer to Carmen. "Can we be of service to you?"

Haemonia glanced around the grotto. "Where is Lady Nemesis and the mortal girl who was wounded?"

"Pluto came for her," replied Carmen.

The sisters gasped at once.

"Pluto came here?" asked Lucina. "We must find Orpheus to commemorate this epic coming in song."

Carmen wasn't listening to the chattering sisters who sounded more like yapping magpies. "I want to leave this place. How do I get out of here?"

"You were brought by a god."

"Well, send a god to come get me."

Lucina glanced at her sisters suspiciously. "Nemesis saved you and brought you. She can take you back. Where is our lady?"

Then from above in the arbor, the birds began to tweet furiously. The sisters turned their eyes and ears skyward, listening.

Lucina narrowed her gaze at Carmen. "You attacked her? You are the Hammer?"

"I am the Hammer," replied Carmen as ribbons of the Veil climbed up her legs, "and I want out of here."

"Sisters," Lucina warned. "Protect the Spring."

"I don't want your stupid water," snapped Carmen. "I want to leave, but if you want to fight, I will oblige."

A pink bolt fired from Carmen's arm as she raised it. It hit Haemonia squarely in the chest, knocking her off her feet.

"Sister!" screamed Euippe, Lucina, and Polyxo together.

They ran to Haemonia's body, but it was too late. The blow from the Hammer had killed their sister instantly. Together, the remaining sisters and all the birds in the trees began to shriek and scream and chatter. The growing din was overwhelming in sound and dimension. Carmen stopped attacking to cover her ears. The noise stung her brain like a million fire ants.

"Stop! I'll kill you all!"

But they didn't. They increased the volume until the very stones of the fountain vibrated. The trees shed their leaves in torrents. The ground ruptured in deep veins. Lucina, Euippe, and Polyxo grabbed onto one another as the vibrations started to destroy the grotto. Suddenly, each of them turned into elegant herons as the sides of the fountain turned to dust and the water drained into the gaping chasms.

Carmen fell to her knees, unable to stand. Around her, the trees sank beneath the shifting earth. The birds had all taken flight and were circling like great schools of fish in the sky. The sisters took to flight and joined the impenetrable gyre above.

Finally, the sound of the birds faded away. Her ears rang with tinnitus, eyes swam with disorienting tears. Carmen put two hands to the earth and found it was stable. She was able to regain her senses after many minutes of recovery only to find herself quite alone on the top of an unknown mountain.

EPIS🌍DE NINE

The Battle of Ancient Livonia

"So, when are you going to tell me the whole story?" asked Calliope as they walked towards the fortified outpost.

"There isn't much time for that right now," said Gunnar. "We have a mission."

"Yes, but we have a little time. I'm dying of curiosity. Besides, you said the guards won't be changing for another hour."

"It takes about that to get inside the outpost through the tunnels."

Calliope was frustrated. "Fine. At least tell me what we're going in there for again. You said it was a…apeshit…or something?

"An aperture," he sighed. "I'm sure you've seen Fletcher's fancy watch. Well, it isn't a watch, it's called an aperture."

"I had photography and graphics class in high school. Aperture was a setting on my camera."

He rolled his eyes. "An aperture opens a hole in the Veil. Big or small, depending on what you need."

"Why haven't you just gotten it before now? Aren't you like a thousand years old or something?" She turned and looked out over the water. "This is all so fucking weird. I wish things would just go back to the way they were just two months ago."

"They will never go back because now you know better."

She turned back to him. "So knowledge made me smarter?"

"It made you just know more. I can't say if you're smarter or not."

"Hey," she let a ball of plasma form in her hand, "watch it."

Gunnar held up his hands surrender-style. "No need to get upset. I know you're a god and we are just starting to learn the extent of your powers."

She flicked the ball towards the water, and it fell like a Roman candle into the waves. "Let me guess, you need me to get us in there because you can't get in by yourself."

"More or less..." he said. "There are a lot of protections."

"Tell me one thing, are you using me? Is that piece of calamari using me, too?"

"No, absolutely not."

She hesitated for just a moment. Something in his tone instantly sent up red flags—when a guy talked like this, needed something from her, led her on, toyed with her—like inviting her for a run and it was just a run. Men suck so hard.

"I will tell you something, I'm fucking having a problem with this. If Squidward is such a god, why can't he just kick Ray's ass on his own..." Her eyes lit up, "...he can't. Because Ray is indestructible. All of you are using me."

"No, it's not like that. You have the tools to help us get the job done. If I could have, I would have done it long ago. We all have a part to play. Look, we need to go if we are going to get there in time." He was desperate to change the subject, "I don't know, to be honest. Are you having second thoughts?"

"I'm not even having first thoughts. You want me to betray a fellow…person…for a giant squid thingy."

"That giant squid thingy wants you to be a queen."

"Bitch, I am already a queen," she snapped. "I don't need you, Ray, or a juiced-up mollusk to be anything. You need me to get off this island, so don't act all surprised that I think you're using me for my power."

"It is true I need you to get off the island in a timely fashion. I would eventually find a way, but here you are. Glad Fletcher brought you so I could teach you this valuable lesson: no one but you has your best interests at heart. I'm honest that I need you to help me escape and I told you. Did Fletcher or his little helper tell you anything or did they lie to you?"

They had never really been straight forward about anything, Calliope conceded. Gunnar was right, no one has her best interests at heart: Ray wants to suck dick, Fletcher wants to have Ray control her, and who know what other agendas she didn't know about. *The Old One was right, why am I playing silly human games. I am the Queen.*

"Let's go and get the aperture, then." He extended his arm, palm up, like a maître-d. "This way, Queen Calliope."

Calliope walked down the ancient fortress stairs, followed by Gunnar. They traversed the innards of the keep until they were deep within and snaked through the passages. After many minutes of descending at a steep decline, the earthen tunnel leveled. Water dripped from the roof, stalactites yawned like teeth. Calliope didn't speak to Gunnar even though he attempted some small talk. He even shared a few personal nuggets, but she wasn't taking the bait. She had a new awareness. It came over her as she mulled the memory of meeting the Old God. If he was so great and magnificent why did he need her? At first, she believed that he wanted her (was *he* even a *he*?) for a queen. For some great partnership between old and new gods.

If he was so ancient and powerful as to not need a name, why did he want a queen? And a human queen at that? One he could not have a royal relationship with. Calliope winced at the thought. She kept walking with Gunnar. What did this guy want? All she knew is that he was a two-face back-stabber to Dr. Fletcher. Calliope didn't have a beef with the doctor, she actually thought he was funny and kind of hot. Did Squidward and Gunnar really think she would become a traitor to another human?

"We're almost there," said Gunnar. "Keep quiet."

"I haven't said anything yet."

She studied him in the gloom. He had a flashlight and there were dim LEDs along the path. Another fucking asshole dude trying to use her. A few small blobs of plasma formed on her nails, further lighting the path. She could just fry him now.

He paused and looked back at her. "Can you put those out. I promise you'll have a chance to use them later."

The plasma faded. Calliope decided she could wait.

Gunnar grinned and turned off his flashlight. The LEDs ceased as they began to ascend into the belly of the outpost. The darkness was thick and impenetrable. Calliope resisted the urge to light up the passage. The guards could be just beyond her sight. They arrived at the end of the tunnel; she felt Gunnar touch her shoulder, signaling her to halt.

Then, in front of them she heard something mechanical. As a crack of light cut the darkness, Calliope saw that Gunnar was opening an ancient iron door with a huge wheel with spokes in the middle. Beyond was a tiny, dim room with another door on the opposite wall.

"What is this place?" whispered Calliope.

"This is an old airlock. About 450 years ago this was covered with water at high tide. This was an escape route for the royal family if they ever needed to do so."

"Did they ever need to do so?"

Gunner hesitated. "No, they died up in the outpost as they ran from the Russians. But that was a long time ago. No more talking."

"How will I know what to do?"

He looked at her flatly. "You're a god. Figure it out."

The next door was actually a false wall, but he seemed to know this already. Gunnar located the hidden trip. As it opened, they exited into an old stone tunnel wired with electric lights. They were equally old. Calliope remembered seeing pictures of World War II in class and thought they looked like those.

Calliope fumed over Gunnar's comment. It was such a dick thing to say. He wasn't any different from the other asshole guys she had encountered before. This time, it burrowed into her brain and nested. *Figure it out.*

In the passage, there was the distant sound of people moving about on the floors above. At the end of the forgotten service tunnel, Gunnar led them into another small room that was more like a broom closet than a passage. Along the far wall was a rusted, flimsy ladder going up to a square of metal in the roof. Gunnar went first and pushed it aside, then disappeared. Calliope followed. With a few other maneuvers, they emerged in an outer garage overlooking the opposite side of the bay housing speedboats and a helicopter.

"We're here," said Gunnar.

"Where do we go now?"

"There's a secure storage vault two floors up in the director's suite. That's where they keep the valuable artifacts and weaponry."

"That's what they think an aperture is? A weapon?"

He looked at her in the eyes. "It opens holes in the universe. It's one of the most powerful weapons there is." He pointed to a bank of elevators. "That's the way up."

Calliope's eyes followed to where he was pointing. "Looks really well-guarded. How are we supposed to get in there without dying?"

"I guess this is when we find out what kind of god you really are." He smiled.

"That's your plan?"

He summoned his atgeir. "I can't die, that's my curse. I don't know about you, but like I said before you are a god. Figure it out so we can get out of here."

A security alarm suddenly echoed through the cavernous room. A few of the Teutonic Order guards pointed in their direction and spoke into their personal earpiece microphones. Protective metal barriers lowered over the windows like falling dominoes. More guards appeared from other directions and fanned out to take defensive positions.

"Motherfucker! OMG I have never been shot at before!" Calliope hissed as gunfire erupted around them. "Are those real bullets?"

"They must have seen us!"

"No shit, what gave you that idea?"

"Take them out!"

Take them out? Calliope screamed as a shower of bullets hit nearby. Pulses of sticky light balls burst to life on her nails, quickly spreading to her hands, then in front of her as a super-heated shield. The instant heat of the sun's plasma melted the bullets in midair and they dropped to the floor. Then there was a long tense silence followed by a bullhorn announcement.

"You are surrounded. There is no escape. Surrender and you will not be killed."

"Not be killed?" Calliope echoed. "I don't want to be killed! This is fucking nuts."

"They're going to kill you anyway," snapped Gunnar. "You think those people want to help you? They want to kill you. They want to kill all gods."

"I thought they were friendly?"

"No, they are all part of The Wire. You know who they are I'm sure of it."

"They attacked us back home. Dr. Fletcher and Nash saved us."

"Fuck them both. They can't save you. Only you can do it."

The bullhorn voice returned. "You have ten seconds to surrender."

"I'm surrendering!" Calliope blurted loudly. "Hold on! I don't want to die!" She stood, hands held high.

"Fucking sit down!" shouted Gunnar. "This is not good."

"Put down your weapons!" the voice boomed.

"I don't have any weapons!" she replied.

"I repeat put down your weapons!"

"Your hands!" hissed Gunnar. "They're glowing. They think you have weapons."

She looked at them. They were alive and sparking with plasma lightning. Calliope focused her will, but she couldn't get them to power down.

"What do I do? I can't get them to stop!" She waved them a little. "They're not weapons! I can't make them go away!"

"Damn it!"

Gunnar stood, and threw his atgeir. His aim was deadly, and he took out the speaker. The atgeir was embedded in the man's chest, only it vanished and rematerialized in Gunnar's grip. He threw it again and skewered another Teutonic Knight.

"Use your power! Or we're dead." The atgeir was again in his hands.

Bullets rang out again. However, the shower of deadly gunfire exploded as it hit a web of heated plasma lightning filling the void between Calliope and the guards. It spread further, spidering through the air. Thunder cracked from the sun-hot heat. The guards didn't stand a chance. As soon as it started, the plasma dissipated. The stench of ozone filled the cavernous space. Calliope collapsed. Exhausted. She figured it out.

Phineas walked across the soft green grass towards the food wagon of Miss Venus. Birds chirped and the summer breeze soothed him. He walked up to the window counter and saw her standing inside. Miss Venus saw him.

"Whiskey?"

He sighed. "Please."

"What brings you here?" she said while she put two shot glasses on the counter and filled them.

"I think I have really fucked things up."

She cackled, "Since when have you not done that?"

"This time it's bad." Phineas paused and looked at Miss Venus. "I know you're not really here, but I have no one else I trust."

"What about Jesse?"

"He is just a child, like the others."

Miss Venus pulled a bag of popcorn off a hook, "He's got part of his father's curse, that boy is hundreds of years old."

"I just left Calliope with his father. I'm hoping he can help her before she destroys herself—and perhaps the world."

"Have you ever thought that she is the destined one rather than Ray?"

"I have. But she wants something from him that he will never be able to give."

"Love?"

Phineas nodded, a little self-defeated. "Like I said, this is just a mess. Maybe the Old Gods will take over and that will be the best solution for this small blue world. We can all just let the Veil sweep us away. I'm getting tired."

"Don't give up so easily. You are being selfish."

"Selfish?"

"This isn't about you winning or losing."

"Is it about evolution?"

"Who knows? The only thing we know so far is human beings are their own worst enemy when it comes to hope. The Old Gods would certainly remedy that by killing them all."

"That is one option, I suppose. Let things go their natural way and not try so hard to manipulate them."

He looked at Miss Venus. The only thing real about this was her memory. He was arguing with himself. Fletcher made some adjustments on his aperture and the image whisked away like blowing ashes from a long cigarette. Fletcher had the whiskey bottle in his hand, though. At least that was real. He was shitty at confrontation and it always ended up in lies that made things even worse.

Time to go back up and speak with the group about what to do next. As much as he dreaded it, he had to tell the truth. He had to fight the urge to lie or minimize because one thing Fletcher hated was being called out and held responsible. As he climbed the stairs, he thought he really had no plan. They all thought he knew everything. He didn't know everything, he was simply very, very old and had seen a lot of bullshit.

Kendall came up from behind Ray. He wrapped his arms around Ray's shoulders, pressing his naked chest against Ray's naked back. For just a moment, Ray flinched and resisted but then he relaxed and accepted the touch. He smiled. It was strange and new, but something he could get used to.

"You okay?" asked Kendall.

"Yeah," replied Ray, "there's just so much to process."

"I guess being a god can be heavy on a guy's shoulders."

Ray turned around, "Actually, that is turning out to be the easy part."

"And this part isn't easy?" Kendall gave Ray a tender kiss, "How is that not easy?"

Ray just grinned. "Don't get me wrong, I think I'm having a hard time processing just how easy it is."

"I never thought about it like that before," said Kendall. "You're talking about coming out, right?"

Ray held up his hands between them. "I never said anything about coming out—yet."

"You seemed to really be enjoying my company."

"That is true," he pushed by Kendall and put on his underwear.

Kendall was already partially dressed and just watched Ray. "God, you are beautiful."

"You're gonna embarrass me," said Ray.

"Oh, come on. You know exactly how hot you are. How can you not?"

"My mom raised me to be humble and that looks and stuff didn't matter."

"OMG they so matter," said Kendall. "One day I'll have a talk with your mom. If we ever get to see our moms again."

Suddenly, there was a knock at the door and Nash stepped in. He surveyed the room. Ray was in his underwear and Kendall was also shirtless. He knew the story in an instant. And smiled.

"Am I interrupting?" he asked.

Ray blushed, startled. "Don't sneak up on us like that. No, you aren't interrupting. Is it time to train or something?"

Nash walked into the room, and he made momentary eye contact with Kendall who just grinned. "I wanted to wish you a happy birthday. Did I miss the party?'

"A little bit," replied Kendall. "Our god boy has had an enlightening birthday so far."

"How so?" asked Nash.

Kendall was about to speak but it was Ray who blurted out the response. "I kissed a boy and I liked it." He laughed. "Katy Perry."

"Yeah, I get it." Nash took a seat on the bed. "So how did all this come about?"

"It started with frosting," said Kendall. "I made him a cake for this birthday and we, um, enjoyed the frosting. But that isn't the most interesting thing that happened."

"What was that?" asked Nash.

Kendall didn't speak, instead he walked over to where Ray was standing. Ray wasn't sure about what was happening, so he turned and faced Kendall who was about a foot away from him. They stood face to face for several moments, giggling like silly kids. Then, Kendall raised his open hand and tenderly placed it on the skin of Ray's perfectly muscular chest.

Nash realized the gravity of the revelation, "Incredible."

He got up and walked over to the boys. He looked at them both, eyes darting from one to the other, daring them to lock with his gaze. Nash lifted his open palm and placed it on Ray's other pectoral muscle. Contact. Skin to skin. Ray turned red in the face, his skin perspired and a sheen fostered the cuts and definitions in his chest.

"You both can touch me." Ray's voice was a sultry whisper.

"Yeah, we can." Nash ran his palm down Ray's chest to his abs. "You can touch us back."

Kendall took his other hand and put it on Nash's shoulder. His caress cascaded down his outer deltoid until it found a lean upper arm. Nash's skin was also hot, perspiration forming, little drips condensing and running down to his fingertips. Ray lifted his hand and touched Nash's bearded face.

"I've never touched a man's beard before."

Kendall smiled, eyes twinkling with mischief. "Ever kiss one?"

"No, you know that." Ray stuttered a little nervously, "Maybe we should take it slow or something..."

"We can take it slow if you want but remember the three of us are together for a long time. And so far, we are the only ones who can touch you, and you can touch us. That's something special." Nash turned his attention to Ray exclusively and stared into his eyes, "We can never tell anyone because it will be too dangerous for me and Kendall. Someone may try to get to you through us because we are the ones who can get beyond your power."

Ray's fingers pressed into Nash's dark beard—coarse, rough, dark, masculine. Then without warning, Ray moved in and put his lips on Nash's. The kiss melted them both, senses spiraled skyward, blood rushing into their penises. Lips gave way to eager tongues, twisting and twining. Breath turned from measured to animalistic panting in a split second. The rush of passion consumed all three of them. As Ray and Nash kissed, Kendall also moved in and the kiss became three. Kendall kissed Ray kissed Nash kissed Kendall kissed Ray kissed Nash. Then the clothes hit the floor.

The shop was quiet upon Fletcher's return. He paused to listen to see if he could detect voices, but the whole place seemed eerily quiet. It unnerved him. This much quiet was unnatural, and always made him suspect things were about to happen. There was silence, too much silence. He was nervous; this deep silence was unnatural for a group of teenagers. There was so much to worry about.

"Hello?" There was no one in the main parlor. "Ray? Jesse?" Something was clearly wrong. "Anyone?"

Fletcher went back to the private room areas and sighed in relief when he heard the sound of voices. The whispers were soft, but filled him with a little warmth for they were familiar. He heard Nash and Ray speaking, and there was a third voice. They were coming from Ray's room. As Fletcher crept closer, he heard the words they said. They were phrases shared by lovers interspersed with pauses and breathing.

Cautiously, Fletcher pushed the door open beyond its small crack to see better. In Ray's bed, were Nash and Ray—and Kendall. They were nude with a tangle of covers about their bodies. Gentle laughter. Kind and tender kisses shared. The world just became more complicated.

Fletcher eased away from the door and made his way back to the main room. His thoughts were muddled. He knew Nash was attracted to Ray, and that it was inevitable for them to hook up. However, seeing Kendall with them was unexpected. It wasn't the fact that they were all three together, it was the disturbing revelation that Nash and Kendall could touch Ray. Fletcher noticed it right away. They were a weakness for him. If anyone knew this, they could exploit it and threaten him. Possibly kill him.

Behind the counter, Fletcher pulled out a shot glass. He still had the bottle of whiskey in his hand from the last visit with Miss Venus. He poured one healthy shot, slammed it, and then poured another for rumination. He'd never felt so out of control of a situation.

"Pour one for me," Poppy said as she entered from the back rooms.

"It's that kind of day," sighed Fletcher as he obliged.

"So, I take it you heard the happy three-way?" Poppy reached up and Fletcher handed her the shot. In her hands it looked like a full-size rock glass.

"The boys need their privacy. They've got a long road ahead of them."

"I suppose so," she said then took a sip of the whiskey. "You missed all the fun."

"What do you mean?"

"Go take a look outside," she said. "While you were away we got a visit from an Old God."

"What?" Fletcher downed his shot.

Then he went to the front door and opened it. He took a few steps out and looked down each side of the street. Debris littered a devastated road. A few cars were overturned. Work crews and police worked the scene.

He stepped back in. "I don't understand how they found us."

"They didn't find the ones with the cloaking runes. I think they found someone else."

"Who?"

"Nemesis."

He said nothing. Fletcher poured one more for himself and slid the bottle away.

"Tell me what happened."

"We heard booms and thought it was a storm or a big truck going by, but it didn't stop. We went to see what it was, and coming down the street, in the clouds, was an Old One. It attacked us hard. You'd be proud of Ray. He really dealt some blows to that thing. But it started shrieking and no one could attack. PJ was hurt really bad. Anyway, Carmen went all Hammer on the thing, flying up in the air, and put it down."

"She has been training…"

"No, this was a display of power and experience. That was no newbie. It was Nemesis."

"I didn't know…"

"…Well know that Carmen disappeared with PJ. Saying there was only one chance to save her…"

He sighed. "Fuck, if it was Nemesis then she took her to the Pierian Spring."

"Only a god would know that."

Just then, Fletcher's phone buzzed signifying a text had arrived. "Hold on."

"What is it?"

He held up a finger to silence Poppy as he read. She watched his eyes, his face, and the jumping muscle in his jaw.

"Well the day just got a little worse. The outpost where I left Calliope was just attacked. I got a message from one of my contacts there."

"Who?"

"Astrid."

"You had something cooking with that bitch?" snapped Poppy.

He sighed. "I had some suspicions, but now I know I wasn't off-base. But I think I may have really fucked up this time."

"What happened?"

"Calliope and Gunnar attacked the base and broke into the vaults."

"WTF!"

Just then, from the back rooms, the three boys joined them. Each had the same expression of afterglow guilt. Fletcher looked at the trio and just sighed. He brought out three more glasses and emptied the bottle.

"Here, you'll want these." He pushed them away from himself as an offering to them.

"Why? What's going on?" asked Nash.

"We were…uh…just training," said Ray.

Kendall nodded. "Training…"

"That's something Nash and I can discuss later," Fletcher looked at his acolyte with a cutting eye. "Right now, we have a huge problem. Calliope has gone rogue with an old friend of mine."

"Friends don't do what he just did," observed Poppy. "And if you thought he was a friend you have some serious qualifier problems."

"True, I consider you a friend." He challenged her gaze, but she looked downward. "For years, hundreds of years, Gunnar has been cursed to that fortress. It is where he sinned against the god Balder who blessed him with victory on the battlefield. Made him impenetrable and gave him a magic weapon to slay his enemies."

"Impenetrable? Like me?" asked Ray.

"No, not in the way you are impenetrable. Kind of like Achilles, who was a real person by the way. In a way, it's my fault he was cursed. There was only one stipulation for Gunnar to live by when he accepted the gift from Balder: do not slay his own flesh in battle. Unknown to Gunnar, the general of the opposing force was the bastard son of his own father—therefore his brother. Gunnar struck him down, and Balder cursed him. As punishment he must live forever and suffer watching all those he loved wither and die over and over again. Eventually he stopped loving anyone. I always visited frequently with him and we became friends. The friendship worked because I wouldn't die on him—at least not anytime soon."

"I don't understand," said Ray. "He was your friend? Is your friend?"

It was Poppy who answered. "What the professor isn't saying is that he knew Gunnar's brother was on the other team and didn't tell him."

Fletcher nodded. "I didn't know how to say it. What to say? I kept it to myself as they went into battle. I thought what are the odds that they would even come in contact. But the bold hero of Livonia, Gunnar, thought the only way to decisively win was to kill their leader. I told him just capture him. Negotiate peace. But Gunnar wanted to be the hero. He wanted that glory so he set out to kill the other guy, and he did."

"So it's not your fault," said Nash. "This is the first time I've heard this whole story."

"How is Calliope involved in this?" asked Ray.

"Even though Gunnar is cursed and an arrogant dick, he is a great warrior. Over the decades he learned patience and I thought he would be a good mentor for her—so she could master her anger. With her power, and her propensity for jealousy and anger, she is a threat to the whole world."

"You talk like she's a monster," said Ray. "She's not a monster, she a fucking teenager like most of us here. Can you imagine what it's like being a teenager and all this shit happening to you."

"True, but if she doesn't get a handle on it…" Fletcher redirected himself. "As I was saying, I've always had a lingering suspicion about Gunnar. Patience can be a weapon in itself. Being able to wait for your opportunity…and I think that's what he did.

"Gunnar is known to the people in Livonia. They know who he is and he's been allowed to exist there. Truth is, they tried to relocate him a few times, but the curse prevented it. As soon as he thought he had escaped the outpost grounds, magically he would find himself right back where he started. Someone even tried to kill him, but it didn't work."

"Was that you?" asked Nash.

"No, besides it didn't work."

Poppy smiled, "It was us…the witches…and with his blessing by the way. But you can't break a god's curse. Only a god can do that." She sighed, "Hence, the reason I am still in this Girl Scout's body."

"Let's stay focused," said Fletcher. "The reason I am telling you this is I believe he was waiting for an opportunity to free himself. That opportunity came in the form of Calliope."

"Can she break a god's curse?" asked Kendall. "I mean, she is a god now, right?"

Fletcher sighed. "Not powerful enough yet. But powerful enough to break into the vaults and steal something that can get around the curse temporarily."

"An aperture," said Nash.

"Yes, an aperture." Fletcher held up his wrist. "This can punch a hole in the Veil. He would be able to escape and stay in the Veil in order to avoid the curse in reality."

"From what I know about the Veil, isn't that just a different kind of prison? As soon as he leaves the bloodstream, he'd be transported back to where he was bound, right?"

"True, but not if he learned how to use a vessel."

"Like Nemesis does," said Kendall. "Cleo explained that to me."

"But Gunnar isn't a god, he can't use a vessel, right?" asked Ray, he was beginning to understand the conversation more and more.

"The universe is a funny place, and we know very little about the Veil. We only know what it wants us to know," said Fletcher. "The Veil will kick your ass in a heartbeat and you will never know why."

"Why are you so worried about Calliope then?" asked Ray.

"Gunnar can't break into the vaults. Nothing, not even his atgeir can do that."

"What's an atgeir?" asked Kendall.

"That's the magic weapon bestowed upon him by Balder the Brave." Fletcher again pulled the conversation back to the original topic. "Gunnar now has access to a god with the firepower to blow open the vaults and get an aperture."

"Calliope?" whispered Ray.

Fletcher nodded, "Yes. Instead of teaching her patience and control, he used his own patience to wait for an opportunity to steal an aperture and escape. Instead, he gave her a taste of the depth of her power. She doesn't need to know patience when she can fry anything and everything. So, that's how I fucked up."

Ray interrupted. "That's why you put her in my school with me. You thought my power would be enough to contain hers? You suck, man."

Fletcher laughed softly, "I guess I do suck, apparently you do now, too, but it was the only way to work with her at the time. It was that or let the Wire murder her. What would be your solution?"

Ray was silent, Fletcher embarrassed him thoroughly.

"That's what I thought," said Fletcher. "But me being my paranoid self and thinking ahead, I asked Astrid to move any apertures or significant artifact weaponry from the vaults."

"So, the vault was empty?" asked Ray.

"Not entirely, but nothing of importance was stored there anymore," replied Fletcher.

"Can we now talk about what happened to PJ?" asked Kendall. "She was hurt really bad in the attack. And she vanished with Carmen. They just poofed away."

Fletcher traded glances with Poppy. "We suspect that PJ was taken to a safe place."

"Well let's go get her," Kendall stood tall. "She was like bleeding from her ears! She needs a hospital."

"She's better off where she is than a hospital," said Poppy.

"Where? Let's go!" exclaimed Kendall.

"We would," said Fletcher apprehensively, "If we knew where it was."

"What does that mean? Where is she?"

"You are really jerking us all around," said Poppy. "I'm the only one with balls enough to say it." She looked at Nash, "I'm sure you would say something, but you got Ray's balls in your mouth."

Poppy was right, thought Kendall. His best friend could be hurt and dying. They were literally prisoners kept in a state of deprivation from the outside world. PJ couldn't defend herself from something like that, and now she was just missing from the world.

Kendall flared angrily. "Man, you are playing some bullshit on us. You keep fucking with us and then never giving us any answers. I'm sick of this. Ray, can we like do a divination thingy and you help me find her?"

Ray was put on the spot. "Um, sure, but I don't know how to do that."

Kendall threw up his hands. "Am I the only one who's had enough?"

Ray raised his hand. Nash reluctantly raised his hand, too. Then Poppy joined them.

"Really?" sighed Fletcher. "Well I'm open to suggestions."

"I got one," said Poppy. "How about we try to locate the Pierian Spring and find PJ? And also maybe try to get Calliope back here. And then think about how we're going to deal with the Old Ones coming back. That sounds like a full meal, now doesn't it?"

"She's right," said Nash. "We're going to get fucked over if we don't realize the Old Ones are sensing an opportunity, like your buddy Gunnar, and plan to come back to take over. I mean, you have an aperture Professor, we can at least go to Livonia and see about Calliope. I've got no clue about the Pierian Spring."

"I can help with that," said Poppy. "Witches are the servants of the Veil."

"That was quick," commented Fletcher. "Since when are you up for things like this? You have been a mystery lately. What are you not saying?"

"Stop being so suspicious," she replied defensively. "You are the one to talk shit about having other motives."

"Touché." Fletcher grinned. "Poppy, I guess you volunteer to find the Pierian Spring. You want to take anyone of these boys with you?"

"Hmmm, I don't want to spoil any *training* sessions," she put air quotes around training and all three of them blushed. "Yeah, you three need to learn to be quiet. I think Kendall would be most helpful to me. If he has a divination, I can read it probably."

Ray was shrinking with embarrassment. "Um…hey…um…" he rang his hands.

"Pay no mind to her," said Nash. "You're a god so you can

pretty much do what you want."

"He is an adult now, too. Or am I the only one who remembered his birthday?" asked Kendall.

"Whatever," sighed Poppy. "I'm just fucking with you. Just get this in your brain right now, you are no better or worse than mortals."

"Got it," said Ray.

"Don't be such a bottom," joked Poppy.

"Hey, we don't sex shame here," added Kendall. "We're sex positive."

Poppy rolled her eyes, "Please get over yourself." She looked at Fletcher, "I need a few hours to prepare to find the spring. You can't leave until then."

"I understand," said Fletcher. He pointed at Nash and Ray, "The two of you gather some things together like clothes and maybe some weapons if you need them. I will come find you when it's time. I need to speak with Poppy privately. Kendall, you go help them and I'll come get you."

"Okay," he grinned. "But knock first."

"Go now," sighed Fletcher. "You exhaust me."

The guys snickered as they left to prepare themselves.

He turned to Poppy. "Talk to me. What's up? You've been hiding something. Where have you been disappearing to? And don't say it's because you were worried about Nemesis coming back. You have never been afraid of Nemesis, even when you were attending her."

"True, it's not about her. But she is back. No doubt. That's how Carmen was able to manipulate the Veil and take PJ away. Carmen is not remotely skilled enough for that."

"Then what's going on?"

"The Earth is singing to my sisters and me. She is anxious and we have been meeting to soothe Her. When She gets agitated, *She* can destroy everything. She just humors us, you know. The true Goddess."

"Yes, the true Goddess. I don't think any of these gods get it that they are here at Her pleasure."

Poppy nodded. "She is generally unbothered by the creatures that live on her skin, but She is tired of being scarred and abused."

"That would make things really bad," he said. "What are the witches planning? You are an elder so you must know something."

"I can't say, but if I am ever allowed to—I will share what I can. Right now, I have to find the Spring." She hesitated, "I hate to say it, but what if PJ is dead?"

"She can't be dead," stated Fletcher. "Let's not even consider that. If she isn't at the Spring then I know of one other place she may be."

"I'll gather what I need. Send Kendall to me in one hour in the lower antechamber where the old ice cream truck is."

The mention of Miss Venus' wrecked and rusted van sent a shiver through him. "Okay."

EPIS☉DE TEN

Happy Birthday, Planet Betty

Poppy sat in meditation when Kendall arrived. It was odd to see her in such a still state. Usually she was a little rage machine spitting sarcasm. Now, however, she was consumed by the faintest of green light, like lightning bug abdomens. Around her there were four candles all within a circle of salt and knitted green willow branches. Was she aware of him? He really didn't want to interrupt her.

"Just sit down and stop staring," she said without opening her eyes.

"How did you know I was here?"

"Your mouth-breathing isn't quiet," she replied. "Now sit down in the circle I prepared for you."

Kendall didn't notice it before, but there was a second salt circle with willow twigs, and four unlit candles in front of Poppy. He went to it and sat; legs folded for meditation. Just as he settled in, the four candles popped to life on their own, startling him.

"There is a bag of ground magical herbs to your left," she said, again without opening her eyes. "Open it. Then take a few strands of your hair or a fingernail or two and put it in. Crush it all up." She waited. "Are you doing it?"

"Hold on," he said. "Jeez give me a second."

"It's not rocket science, pretty boy," she said.

"There's the Poppy I know and love." Kendall jerked a few hairs from his head and peeled off the tip of his pinky nail. "Okay, I'm putting it in the bag now. And I'm mixing it all together."

"Now pour it in front of you in the form of a pentagram."

Kendall opened the bag. "Wait, do you mean a pentagram pointing towards me or towards you?"

Poppy sighed. "If you point it towards yourself it will be upside down and you'll go to hell, okay?"

Kendall gulped. "So the point is towards you."

"Yes, the point is towards me. It should look like a star."

He sifted the powder out of the bag in the form of a star in front of himself. It began to glow the soft green that bathed Poppy. Then it lifted and dispersed around his own body. He was glowing just like she was.

"That feels weird," he commented. "Like ants on my body."

"It is Mother Earth embracing you. The essence you placed in the mix let Her know who you are." She raised her right arm, palm up, and extended her left arm towards the ground, palm down. "Do like I am doing."

Kendall obliged. He had so many questions just a second ago, but they abandoned his mind as the glow enrobed him. He watched as Poppy pixelated and turned transparent. He looked down at his legs crossed in front of him. They, too, were translucent and passing away like blowing ashes.

As the world seemed to trade places with another, Kendall could still see Poppy sitting in front of him. They were moving through time and space. Features of the room were replaced with a deep forest of trees and dappled sunlight. A scent of honeysuckle and lilacs played on the breeze. Birds sang friendly songs and colorful insects whirled. His body solidified in this new space.

In front of him, Poppy opened her eyes. "We're here."

"What was that?" asked Kendall, trembling from the rush of energy.

"We traveled."

"That's impossible. Where are we really?"

"We are in the embrace of Mother Earth." She stood, "You can get up now." Her candles extinguished on their own.

Kendall also stood and his candles went out. Poppy began to walk through the deep forest. He followed in silence, just taking in all that he was experiencing. Kendall still had the green glow bathing his body as did Poppy. Tiny creatures came to check them out as they continued their journey. Soon, they entered a clearing where there were other figures around a pool of water.

"Is this the Spring?"

"No, it isn't the Spring. We're somewhere else."

"Wait I thought we were supposed to find Carmen and PJ at the magic spring."

"Be quiet, asshole."

"Hey…"

"…I said shut up. Don't interrupt."

An older woman noticed Poppy approaching and turned her attention to them. "Sister."

"Sister," replied Poppy. "I see you were able to bring an oracle. Very good."

"Bring an oracle?" Kendall stopped in his tracks. "I thought we were here to find the spring."

"I shall summon Etienne, she will be happy there is an oracle." They spoke as if he wasn't even there.

"Have there been any changes?"

"Not yet," the older sister replied. "The oracle will be able to tell us, perhaps."

"Perhaps?" he said rhetorically. "Hello? I'm right here. You can talk to me."

Finally, Poppy looked at him. "Will you please stop embarrassing me? You are here to help us. To help Mother Earth."

"What does she need my help for?"

Poppy sighed and rolled her eyes, "Goddess help me."

Then, from out of the misty trees stepped an imposing figure. She was at least seven feet tall, slender, and lipstick red. She wore the gauzy fabric of the others present but commanded the area with her imposing presence. As Etienne drew closer, Kendall saw that she was reptilian with yellow eyes that blinked vertically. He was totally creeped out and didn't want to stare at her.

"Greetings, Poppy," she said with a harmoniously soft voice. "Thank you for bringing us an oracle. Hopefully, we can get some answers."

"Hey, I'm already spoken for. I'm an oracle for Ray—you know the god."

"Yes, the indestructible boy." Etienne walked over to Kendall, towering over him, and placed a gentle scaly red claw upon his shoulder. "Do not worry, he is your god. However, all oracles also have a deep connection to Mother Earth and to the bloodstream of the universe. It is the Veil that gives you the visions."

"I don't know about that," said Kendall skeptically.

"You won't be harmed, and you will not be required to do anything against your god. However, only an oracle for a strong god such as Ray can be the one to help us—if at all. Poppy has told us all about you and your group of friends."

"She has, has she?" Kendall cut his eyes at her. "Gurl, that is so shady."

"Shut up, dork," snapped Poppy. "You can't tell anyone I brought you here, got it?"

"Why not? Will Dr. Fletcher get pissed at you?"

"Ah, Phineas Fletcher," smiled Etienne. "He is an old friend and not a worry."

"Then why all the secrecy? Why not just ask me?"

"True," said Etienne. "We were unsure if you would feel your loyalty would be threatened. Or perhaps, you would say no because of it."

"Just tell me what you want me to do, and then let me decide."

Etienne double-blinked quickly. "The only thing you have to do is wade into the Pierian Spring and let us read any divination that occurs."

"Wait, this is the Pierian Spring—the magic spring?"

Etienne nodded. "I know you are seeking it, but this is not the instance of the Spring you are looking for."

"What does that mean?"

"The Pierian Spring exists in time and space, many at once. The one you seek is protected by the Pierides—the daughters of King Pieria. There were four daughters at that spring, and as you see around you the other 5 are here. However, there has been a tragedy. There was an attack, but we don't know much about what happened. One sister has been killed. The remaining sisters have hidden the Spring away so to protect it from whomsoever attacked."

"I know who attacked it," said Kendall. "It was Nemesis. Or Carmen. One of them."

The news troubled Etienne. "How do you know this? Nemesis is a god. She would be unlikely to attack a sacred fountain. She has bathed in this fountain many, many times."

"Then it was Carmen," said Kendall. "She's the Hammer. Or something like that. Something about the Veil."

Etienne turned to Poppy, "Do you know of this?"

She nodded. "I was there when the Old God attacked. I suspected Nemesis was using Carmen as a vessel, yet she had not made herself known."

"…And this Carmen? She is the Hammer of the Veil?"

"I have been at all her tests and trainings," said Poppy. She lowered her eyes, "I'm sorry I did not say anything sooner."

"We will have to address your purposeful omissions later, but for now it seems we have an unstable person commanding the powers of the bloodstream." She sighed heavily, "I fear your lack of exposition may have caused us great harm, Poppy."

"I have no excuse," she said.

Etienne returned her attention to Kendall. "Please, step to the Spring and enter it."

"How deep is it? Is it safe?" He looked at the inky dark water, "I've never seen purple and pink water before."

"It is safe, you are a chosen oracle. Mother Earth will accept you."

"What if she doesn't?"

"Get in the fucking water, Kendall. Before I push you in." snapped Poppy.

Apparently, the tactic was successful. He swallowed hard and climbed up on the lip of the fountain. He took off his clothes and stood naked in front of everyone, unashamed. The stones were grey and ancient, about two feet wide and three feet tall. He couldn't see any stairway, so he simply stepped out. His foot entered the water, and it was surprisingly buoyant. An instant sense of trust filled him. Mother welcomed him.

Kendall sank down to his waist and sat. He closed his eyes, sighed, and allowed the blood to wash over his body. Purple. Pink. Lavender. Soft. Tender.

Then Etienne spoke: "You are in the heart of this earth. Feel Her pulse. She is just one sister in the sisterhood of worlds linked by the bloodstream of the universe."

He lowered his head. Kendall did not hear Etienne talking. In his mind, he heard a gentle harmonic sigh of notes. So gentle that if he concentrated, he could not hear it; but if he just let it flow the sound was audible. A smile kissed his lips. In the spring, the water swirled and created new hues. Some were warm. Some were cool. Kendall settled into full lotus position as the water currents probed his body. Then, he felt the sensation of weight in his lap. It didn't startle him. In fact, it was soothing. He was waking from the trance.

"Wow," he whispered. "That was amazing."

He felt the weight still in his lap and reached down to touch it. There was an object about the size of a basketball, but oblong and slimy. He caressed it, nurturing it.

"Hey," he attempted to turn his head and look back at the others. "What happened? Guys, there is something in my lap."

Etienne walked to the edge. "Dear oracle, you have shown us so much. How can we thank you?"

"What did you see?"

"You have been in a trance-state for nearly three hours," said Etienne. "You have shown us many divinations on your flesh. We know what Mother Earth desires of us."

"But what about this?" He turned on his rear so he could face everyone, but still stayed submerged. "This thing just appeared in my lap." He held it gingerly in his arms, cradled it, and brought it to the surface. "What is it?" Etienne, Poppy, and all the attendants gasped. "What?"

In his arms was a sanguine-colored orb, marbled with veins of white light. The egg began to open along the seams, its occupant pushing out into the world. Kendall looked down at it. He wasn't shocked nor did he feel threatened. Instead, he held it close as the hatching continued.

A slender tentacle eased out of one crack and slithered up around Kendall's neck. A piece of the shell fell away as another tendril emerged and wrapped around Kendall's neck.

"Someone do something!" shouted Poppy. "It's trying to kill him." She powered up her magic.

"No," Etienne calmed her, "look."

More of the shell fell away into the water leaving a tiny, slimy squid-like creature nestled in Kendall's arms. It was embracing him back and made a soft cooing noise. On either side of its head were enormous eyes that were not yet opened.

Kendall smiled, tears in his eyes. "I think I'm a mama."

Calliope ran her hand along the seam of the reinforced steel of the vault. It was the last of three. The others were conspicuously empty of contraband of any significance, according to Gunnar. She didn't know what she was looking for, but she was quite enjoying breaking and melting things. Calliope laid a bead of plasma, stood back, and let it ignite. However, this vault was especially stubborn.

"This has to be the one," said Gunnar. "Peculiar that the others had nothing of real value. This is one of the major outposts on the planet."

"Maybe they knew we were coming," proposed Calliope.

"They are not that brilliant. I have been watching them for hundreds of years. They are egotistically blind to everything, these Scholars. They think they are so smart."

"What do we do?"

"Just blast it open." He moved away a safe distance.

"What if more knights show up?"

Gunnar looked down the hall. "I doubt it. We killed many of them and hurt the rest. They are too scared to come after me."

"Why don't you see if you can open it with that spear?"

"My atgeir cannot open this sealed vault. I've tried before."

Calliope stopped when he said that. "You've tried this before? How many times?"

"A few. It doesn't matter. Just blow it."

"I'm starting to think you're using me to get into this vault because you can't do it yourself."

"If you don't hurry up, we will certainly get caught. We need to get that aperture and get the hell out of here before reinforcements show up."

"You can just kill them, too," she said. "Or I can just blast them all. We took this place over."

"We haven't taken this place over. We had the element of surprise, and we will be caught if you don't open that vault."

Calliope sighed. Men. Fucking men. Using her. Embarrassing her. Choosing another guy over her. Fuck them. Angrily she pushed a blast of plasma into the door and it exploded in a sizzling, radiating, melting rage. A gaping hole stood in the wake of her anger.

"Thank you," said Gunnar. "Come on, let's get out of here."

They entered the vault. There were boxes along the far wall, and a couple of cabinets with chains on them. The apertures had to be in one of those. Gunnar summoned his atgeir and easily sliced open one of the cabinets. Inside were a hodgepodge of trinkets and antiques but none were apertures. He went to a second cabinet and cut the chain off the door. He pulled them open and began to inspect the contents. Again, there was nothing of importance inside.

"We don't have fucking time to go through every box," he anxiously said. "Blast them open."

"What if I destroy them?"

"What have we got to lose?" he said. "If we can't use one to escape, we're dead."

"Maybe you are," said Calliope. "I'm not cursed to this island."

"Don't even think about double-crossing me, sweetheart," warned Gunnar.

"What are you going to do? I can just walk out of here."

He turned his atgeir on Calliope. "I will kill you where you stand."

Calliope powered up, summoning plasma balls that grew in front of her. Gunnar threw the atgeir at her, but lightning erupted as the steel impacted her energy. Fucking men. The atgeir vanished and returned to Gunnar's hand, however it was white-hot from the electricity that had roasted it. He shrieked as his hand burned, seared to the metal. He had to concentrate on releasing the weapon and it clattered to the metal floor.

She stepped back towards the doorway, "I am so out of here."

Calliope ran down the hall, towards the immense room below. It was a smoking disaster. She gasped. There were dead bodies on the floor amongst the ruins. She did that. She killed them.

Truly, Gunnar must have killed some of them, but not all of them. With her power, she murdered them.

Then, as she stood staring at the carnage, a bright light erupted and three familiar humans came through: Phineas Fletcher, Jesse Nash, and Ray Kellan. Although she could not hear them, from their body language she could tell they were in shock. Ray rushed to a fallen body near them, checked for life, but shook his head. He pointed to another one near Nash and he also checked for life. Fletcher scanned the room and saw her.

"Calliope!" he shouted. "Please, stop what you are doing. You're hurting people. This is not you!"

Ray looked up and saw her, too. "Calliope! Please!"

He didn't wait for a response and bolted across the floor in her direction. As he ran, the golden shield stretched around his body, elongating with every stride, lifting him in the air. Behind Calliope, Gunnar appeared with his atgeir. He threw it at Ray, but it deflected harmlessly away.

"Stop!" screamed Calliope. "Everyone stop!"

Her power swelled like a tidal wave, engulfing the entire area. Calliope's plasma fried everything it touched, except for Ray's shield. He pushed back at her, containing her power. Angrily, Calliope concentrated on making more energy. Blast everything. Make them all stop. All these men. *Fuck these men.*

Then, the clash of god power overwhelmed the human building in which they fought. Plasma and shield compressed and rebounded in a shock wave that tore the building to shreds. Nothing was spared. Shrapnel rained down on the sea, sizzling and steaming as it hit the cool Baltic waters. The vault of Livonia was destroyed.

ABOUT THE AUTHOR

STEVEN LEE CLIMER is a born creative and works in the written, visual, and aural arts. He has been writing fantasy, horror, and science fiction for kids of all ages, for over 30 years. He is the author of 15 novels, including the award-winning *Dream Thieves*, and *Demonesque,* which was optioned for a feature film.

His short stories have appeared in print and online publications in North America and the UK. Steven is also an accomplished acrylic and oil painter, and when not writing and painting, Steven composes chill EDM music under the name SugarBuzz. His music can be experienced on Spotify, Apple Music, iHeartRadio, and Amazon Music. He believes there are different voices and moods for each creative medium—like family harmony. He lives with the love of his life in Philadelphia, and they are the proud dads of a porkie named Rocky and two cats.